D0295831

UB

ITEM

New York City Docs

*Hot-shot surgeons,
taking the world by storm...
by day and by night!*

In the heart of New York City, four friends
sharing an apartment in Brooklyn are on
their way to becoming the best there is at the
prestigious West Manhattan Saints Hospital—
and these driven docs will
let *nothing* stand in their way!

Meet Tessa, Kimberlyn, Holly and Sam
as they strive to save lives and become
top-notch surgeons in the Big Apple.
Trained by world-class experts,
these young docs are the future—and they're
taking the medical world by storm.

But with all their time dedicated to patients,
late nights and long shifts, the last thing they
expect is to meet the loves of their lives!

For fast-paced drama and sizzling romance,
check out the *New York City Docs* quartet:

Hot Doc from Her Past
Tina Beckett

Surgeons, Rivals...Lovers
Amalie Berlin

Falling at the Surgeon's Feet
Lucy Ryder

One Night in New York
Amy Ruttan

Available from February 2016!

Dear Reader,

Our family lived and worked for many years in Brazil. One of the most fascinating things we experienced while we were there was our son's class doing a demonstration of *capoeira*, a Brazilian martial art. It was completely different from what I'd expected, with its flowing movements accompanied by the beat of tambourines and a unique instrument called a *berimbau*.

In *Hot Doc from Her Past*, Dr Tessa Camara is slogging through the last year of her residency along with three other housemates. Tessa happens to have Brazilian parents, who have encouraged her to retain bits and pieces of her heritage—one of which is *capoeira*. When her martial arts studio decides to participate in the hospital's summer festival it creates the perfect storm—because an old flame has just burst back into her life…someone she is desperately trying to steer clear of. Only the hospital, her friends and fate have other plans!

Thank you for joining Tessa and Clay as they circle each other in the *capoeira* ring and in life, each hoping to avoid losing not only the match but also their hearts. I hope you enjoy reading their story as much as I loved writing it!

Love

Tina Beckett

HOT DOC
FROM HER PAST

BY
TINA BECKETT

First published in Great Britain 2015
By Mills & Boon, an imprint of HarperCollins*Publishers*
1 London Bridge Street, London, SE1 9GF

Large Print edition 2016

© 2015 Tina Beckett

ISBN: 978-0-263-26074-8

Printed and bound in Great Britain
by CPI Antony Rowe, Chippenham, Wiltshire

A three-time Golden Heart finalist, **Tina Beckett** is the product of a Navy upbringing. Fortunately she found someone who enjoys travelling just as much as she does and married him! Having lived in Brazil for many years, Tina is fluent in Portuguese and loves to use that beautiful country as a backdrop for many of her stories. When not writing or visiting far-flung places Tina enjoys riding horses, hiking with her family and hanging out on Facebook and Twitter.

Books by Tina Beckett

Mills & Boon Medical Romance

Hot Brazilian Docs!
To Play With Fire
The Dangers of Dating Dr Carvalho

One Night That Changed Everything
NYC Angels: Flirting with Danger
The Lone Wolf's Craving
Doctor's Guide to Dating in the Jungle
Her Hard to Resist Husband
His Girl From Nowhere
How to Find a Man in Five Dates
The Soldier She Could Never Forget
Her Playboy's Secret

Visit the Author Profile page at millsandboon.co.uk for more titles.

To those who hold two countries in their hearts.

Praise for Tina Beckett

'…a tension-filled emotional story with just the right amount of drama. The author's vivid description of the Brazilian jungle and its people make this story something special.'
—*RT Book Reviews* on
Doctor's Guide to Dating in the Jungle

'Mills & Boon Medical Romance lovers will definitely like *NYC Angels: Flirting with Danger* by Tina Beckett—for who *doesn't* like a good forbidden romance?'
—*HarlequinJunkie*

CHAPTER ONE

Twelve years earlier

THERÉSIA CAMARA SAT cross-legged on her bedroom floor surrounded by clothes. Someone else's clothes. Two huge garbage bags full, to be exact. She glanced down at the brand-new sundress she'd worked ten hours to buy and felt sick. What had seemed like an extravagant purchase two days ago—one that had made her feel grown-up and independent—looked cheap when compared with the designer labels on what she'd just been given.

And how could she not wear them? Worse, how could she not be utterly grateful that her best friend had thought of her when sorting through her closet? There were more clothes in those two sacks than she'd ever owned.

What it made her feel, though, was poor.

She swallowed. It was okay. She'd make good

use of them, including the plum-colored prom dress tucked inside a boutique garment bag that now hung on the back of her closet door. No one would remember that Abby had worn it last year, right?

Tessa's parents—who'd worked hard ever since moving from Brazil to the United States—were just getting their painting and remodeling business off the ground. In fact, they'd recently secured a huge contract with a Manhattan firm, redoing a group of office buildings, a project that would keep them busy for the next few years, if the owner was happy with the first batch. But there were materials and supplies to buy in preparation for the work. They certainly didn't have the money to buy her a fancy party dress she would wear only once. Or clothes in preparation for her senior year in high school, which started in two short weeks.

She straightened her back and picked up a pair of dark-wash skinny jeans that were almost new. Luckily she and her friend were the same size. This was a godsend really, and she would see it for what it was. It would take a load off her parents—which was also the reason she'd sought a job stocking the shelves at a local supermarket to help ease their burden. There would be enough expenses as it was, with graduation and applying for scholarships for college. And then medical school. She crossed her fingers and kissed them in the hope that this particular dream came true.

And someday... She brought the jeans to her chest and squeezed them tight, her heart filling with hope. Someday *she* would be the one helping others. She was going to work harder than she ever thought possible to make sure her grades stayed as high as they were now. Then she would see that her parents were taken care of—even if their new contract went bust. It was what they'd done for her by moving to a new country. And she did have everything she needed, even if those things didn't come from exclusive stores.

Tessa didn't need labels. Or a ton of money. She just needed to succeed, no matter what sacrifices she had to make. As of now, she was making a pact with herself. She was going to get through school on her own. Without any help.

From anyone.

CHAPTER TWO

"*Domingo, Segunda-feira, Terça-feira, Quarta-feira...*" Reciting the days of the week in Portuguese had always helped center her before. But as Tessa continued to enunciate each syllable of each word, the bubble of horror that was trapped in her throat refused to burst. Instead, it grew larger with every breath.

She stared at the huge cardboard placard propped on an easel in the lobby of West Manhattan Saints, the one welcoming the hospital's newest orthopedic surgeon.

People swerved to avoid her as they made their way into the medical facility, and one man bumped her shoulder with a muttered apology about being late as he passed her. Tessa was running late, too, but at the moment she was powerless to do anything except stand there.

Clayton Matthews, a blast from the past—*her*

past—sported the same lazy half smile she knew so well. The one that tipped up one corner of his mouth and made everything inside her liquefy. And he seemed to be aiming that smile squarely at her, and in turn at everyone who might stop to gaze upon him.

Ha! *Gaze upon him.* That made him sound like a god or something.

He had been godlike to her at one time. Before she'd realized exactly who had provided her "scholarship" to medical school. The one that had paid for almost her entire education.

Not him. But his parents. She had no idea why they had, other than the fact that her parents and Clay's had become fast friends as her mom and dad worked on a huge block of Clay's dad's buildings. Her dad was still in partnership with them, as a matter of fact.

That partnership was how she'd met Clay in the first place. And the placard brought that last terrible scene on graduation night rushing back.

She swallowed. *God.* She did not want to face him. Especially now. Not with the second anniversary of her mother's death weighing on her mind.

So she wouldn't. This final part of her residency was in cutaneous oncology—another reminder of her mom's courageous battle—while Clay was an orthopedic surgeon. They would be on different floors, even. How likely was it that they would really run into each other in the huge hospital?

Taking a deep breath, she let herself relax slightly.

"Wow, Tessa, you look like you've just seen a ghost." Holly Buchanan, one of the housemates at the Brooklyn brownstone where she lived, stopped beside her. Long brown locks shifted to the left as the other woman tilted her head and looked at the poster. "Ooh, although he's not a bad-looking ghost. Is that the newest member of our happy family?"

Tessa's mouth twisted in a wry grimace. Happy? With the grueling hours they were putting in on the final year of their residency, no one had much time to notice the general atmosphere around the teaching hospital. Harried and exhausted described most of the people Tessa knew. That included her female housemates, Holly and

Caren, and her one male housemate, Sam, who lived in the other three units at the brownstone. The friends saw each other more at the hospital than they did at the house.

"I guess he is." She did her best to stifle the bitter edge to her voice, but something must have come across.

"Do you know him?" Holly's shoulder nudged hers.

"No." Because it was true. The man she had thought she'd known had been nothing like the man he'd turned out to be. "No, I don't know him. At all."

It had been how long? A little over four years. Besides, he was married now, at least that's what she'd heard.

A warm scent tickled her nose, just as a warning tingle lifted the fine hairs on her neck.

"I think 'at all' might be stretching the truth, don't you think, Tess?" That voice. Mellow. Matching the half smile on the poster to a T. "Because I *definitely* know you."

She wrenched her body around to face the newest threat, just as he held out his hand to

Holly. "Clayton Matthews, Orthopedics, nice to meet you."

Holly's eyes widened as they flicked to meet hers, and then she accepted Clay's proffered hand and murmured her own name and specialty. Tessa sent out a desperate plea to her housemate that was summarily ignored.

"Well, I need to get back to work," her friend said, "before Langley takes me down. Again."

The head of surgical residents, Gareth Langley didn't suffer fools lightly, and somehow he and Holly had gotten off to a rocky start. Tessa steered clear of the man whenever possible.

Her housemate then slipped from between them and hurried down the hallway, blinking out of sight as she rounded the corner to the elevators. That left her alone with Clay. And his poster.

"Tessa, good to see you again. How are you?"

Really? That was the best he could do, after everything that had gone on between them? "Fine. You?"

"Surprised." A flash of teeth accompanied that word. "I had no idea you were doing your residency at West Manhattan Saints."

Didn't he? Since West Manhattan was one of the biggest teaching hospitals in the city, how could he not realize this was where she'd wind up?

Unless he really had known and had come here to torment her.

Delusional, Tess. That's what you are. He did not follow you to this hospital.

She decided to ignore his comment, nodding at the placard instead. "Nice likeness."

The impulse to start counting days again winked through her head…this time in English. She fought the urge. And the picture *was* nice. It showed off his thick black hair, strong chin, those deep blue eyes that could slide over you and make you think you were the only person in the world.

Even when you weren't.

At least it was only a head shot, because from the chest down he was no less mouthwatering than he'd been four years ago—something she was doing her damnedest not to dwell on.

He glanced at the picture. "You do what you have to. You should know that better than anyone."

Yes, she did. Like continue working your heart

out when you discovered your so-called free ride hadn't actually been free at all. And that the man standing in front of her had known where things stood the whole time they'd shared classes…when they'd become an item. When he'd laid her down on the bed in his dorm room and become her very first lover.

Then had come the gifts. Small at first. Then more expensive, despite her protests.

It had all blown apart at her graduation cere- mony when he'd handed her a flat jeweler's box with a kiss and murmured congratulations. A half hour later she'd learned over a loudspeaker that the Wilma Grandon Memorial Scholarship had actually been named after Clay's maternal grandmother and that Tessa had been its one and only recipient.

A thousand eyes had swiveled in her direction.

At that moment, she'd been transported back to her childhood bedroom and those sacks of used clothes. Only this was much, much worse. Once again, she was the poor immigrant girl from Brazil who had nothing. Waves of humiliation washed up her face and flooded her body. How could he do that to her?

The embarrassment ignited, turning into something else that scorched across her soul. Only this time the passion she'd inherited from her homeland turned everything inside her to a barren wasteland.

Tessa sent his parents a warm thank-you letter, expressing her gratitude. She sent Clay a completely different kind of letter—returning his graduation present and telling him it was over. That she needed to concentrate on her residency. She repeated that refrain when he showed up at her dorm room—not letting him see how gutted she was that he'd kept such a huge piece of information from her. He evidently bought the excuse, because it was the last time she'd seen him.

Until now. But at least she could be cordial to him. Maybe he would take the hint, and they would settle on polite indifference in any future encounters.

She held out her hand, as he'd done to Holly moments earlier. "Well, it's good to see you again, Clay. I hope you like it here."

There was a moment's hesitation, and then he took her hand, his palm skimming across hers in a heart-stopping combination of warmth and friction as his fingers closed around hers.

Heat poured into her belly and rushed up her face.

Too late she realized her mistake. Because this was no squeeze-and-release grip. This was intimate—a connection that went far beyond the physical realm—and her body reacted to the promise it brought along with it.

A shiver ran over her as he drew her a step closer. "I think I already do."

She blinked for a second before realizing his words were in response to hers…that she hoped he'd like it here.

How bad would it be if she turned tail and ran right back out of the hospital, abandoning everything she'd worked so hard for?

Very bad. She was here for a specific reason. To treat those with skin diseases that were sometimes benign—and sometimes deadly.

She wasn't going to run. Not from anyone. Time

to nip whatever this was in the bud. She tossed her head as the perfect solution came to mind.

"I heard you got married. How's your wife?" She allowed a little acid to color her voice as she gave her hand a slight tug, hoping he'd take the hint.

He did. But not before his thumb skimmed over the back of her wrist in a way she recognized. Her temper died as her heart cracked in two. How could he do this?

"She's not my wife anymore." His throat moved as if he suddenly needed to swallow. When he spoke again, there was a rough edge to his voice. "We're divorced."

Divorced. Oh, God. How was she going to survive if she ran into him every day?

"I'm sorry to hear that. But I'm running late…"

Maybe he heard the frantic words that were echoing in her brain, because he took a step back, his expression cooling. "I'll let you go, then. I'm sure we'll see each other around the hospital."

Whether it was a threat or a promise, she had no idea, but she saw her opportunity and grasped it with both hands, throwing him a quick, empty smile and walking away from him as fast as her legs could carry her.

And yet he watched her go. She could feel his gaze on her back, and from the heating of her hindquarters she wondered if those blue eyes had skimmed over that part of her, as well.

Divorced. Oh, how much easier it would have been if he was happily married with a van full of squawking progeny.

What had happened between him and his wife? He hadn't sounded all that happy that his marriage was over.

It's none of your business, Tessa. She quickened her steps, switching into what she called waddle mode—when her pace became too fast for her legs to handle and the wiggle of her hips shifted into overdrive.

But, waddle or not, she had to get away from him. And stay away. At least until the end of her current residency cycle. Maybe she should rethink her plans of applying for that Mohs micrographic surgery fellowship here at West Manhattan. She could always move to another teaching facility.

But she loved it here. Loved the hospital. Loved living in the brownstone with Sam, Caren and Holly. Was she really going to let Clay drive her out?

She turned the corner, but she didn't slow down until she was on the elevator and heading toward the third floor. Then she sagged against the wall.

Clayton Matthews. Here in her hospital.

Her lips tightened. No. She was here to stay. She'd been toying with getting her own place and possibly even starting a family once her residency was done—a huge decision, but one she'd been thinking about for a while. She wasn't going to drastically alter her course, no matter how much he made her insides melt. He'd lost none of his sizzle factor, she'd give him that.

So she was going to continue doing the things she loved as if she'd never seen him—although she had no idea how that was possible. She'd just have to come up with some kind of strategy for future sightings.

The doors to the elevator swished back open, and she stepped out onto the busy floor of the world she knew and loved.

Strategy.

She mulled that word over for a second or two before discarding it. Right now, she would practice *preventative* medicine. If it worked in health care, it could surely work in her love life—not that she had one. Since Clay, she'd dated two men. Neither had lasted more than a couple of months. She could never seem to relinquish enough control to make a steady relationship work.

Okay. So *prevention* was the word of the day—the word for avoiding negative consequences. Starting now, Tessa would practice prevention when it came to Clay.

Which meant avoiding him. At all costs.

"Traditional Capoeira of Brazil."

The familiar name on the list of businesses supporting the hospital's annual summer Health Can Be Fun festival caught Clay's eye. At the bottom of the page were hundreds of lines—many already filled in with the names of volunteers. Hospital staff had been encouraged to find a place to serve ahead of the July 19 event. Most of the easier tasks—like raffle drawings, the ticket booth and kiddie face painting—were taken. He shook his head. He'd have to look at it again when he was a little calmer.

Seeing Tessa this morning had thrown him for a loop. Maybe he would have handled it better had she not been standing in front of that ridiculous poster the hospital had insisted on putting up. But there she'd been, talking with one of her friends. His gut had tightened when he heard the other woman laugh at something Tessa said. Because there'd been nothing funny about what had happened between the two of them.

And when Tessa denied knowing him…

Well, that had been the last straw. Any thought of sliding by the pair unnoticed had fled in a rush of anger.

Except he'd seen something flit through Tessa's eyes when she turned and saw him standing there. Dismay? Horror? Guilt? He couldn't place what it had been exactly, but he refused to believe what had come to mind when he'd first seen that look: pain.

There'd been no pain in the tight lips and steady gaze on the day he'd shown up on her doorstep, only to have her confirm they were through. If anyone should have felt pain back then, it had been him. Things had been tense between them for the last six months of their relationship, but he'd never dreamed she'd been that unhappy. Unless it had been about the money all along. Except she'd returned his bracelet.

His teeth clenched until his jaw ached. He'd been over and over this years ago and had come up empty.

Someone else came into the lounge and cleared her throat, making him realize a woman was waiting, pen in hand, to sign up for something. He took a couple of steps back and let her take his place.

His gaze cut back to the name of the local *capoeira* studio. Did Tessa still train there? When they'd been together, she'd sent him a handwritten invitation, asking him to come and learn a little more about her Brazilian heritage. He'd accepted without hesitation. And it had been worth it. Watching her work out inside the circle they called a *roda* had been beyond sexy—the intricate, flowing moves had highlighted the lean lines of her body and made *capoeira* look more like a dance than a true martial art.

He'd soon learned differently. It was just as passionate and fiery as Tessa was—and just as proud.

He shook himself back to the present as the attractive brunette finished writing her name and turned toward him with a smile, her dark eyes skipping over him. "Thanks. Better get in there and choose something. Pickings are getting mighty slim."

"So it would seem." He managed to return her smile, although the last thing he wanted to do was engage in small talk with a member of the opposite sex. He'd been burned twice now. Maybe he should have become a priest, like his cousin.

Except he did like women. He just didn't have the knack for long-term relationships, evidently. That was one gene his parents—married for thirty-five years now—hadn't passed down to him.

"See ya," the brunette said with yet another smile, although she didn't try to introduce herself, as Tessa's friend had. He was just as glad.

"Yep. Good luck with that." He nodded toward the board.

"You, too. Maybe we'll wind up volunteering for the same thing."

That was probably meant as a hint, but since Clay hadn't even noticed what she'd signed up for, she was out of luck. "Maybe."

She exited the room, leaving Clay to stare at the sheet again and wonder about Tessa and the studio. Especially when he looked closer and noticed that she hadn't signed up for anything, either, although the list of businesses didn't have slots for sign-ups. They must be using their own people in the rented booths.

It didn't matter. How hard could an hour or two of volunteer work be? He could always sign up for the cleanup crew, which still had several time periods available. That way he wouldn't have to interact with anyone.

But right now all he wanted to do was get to work and forget about his encounter with a certain redhead.

Except that a few parts of Clay were still smoldering from seeing her again. Time to remedy that. The sooner he could locate his mental fire extinguisher and douse those areas with a mixture of foam and water, the better it would be. For both of them.

CHAPTER THREE

WHERE WAS HIS EX-WIFE?

Clay sat in the hospital cafeteria with Molly and listened to his daughter chatter on about all she'd done with Grandma and Grandpa yesterday evening. He couldn't hold back a sigh as she bounced in her chair and scooped up a bite of fruit from her plate.

His parents had been stoic all during his divorce, although they must have been disappointed in him for not working harder to make things work. He'd tried. Hell, he'd never expected his marriage to end in divorce any more than they had. But nothing he'd tried had worked. He'd compromised on where he'd practiced medicine to be closer to the house. He'd taken on the bulk of Molly's care when she'd been a baby. He'd even gone to marriage counseling.

And yet here he sat.

His biggest failures in life, it seemed, had to do with women.

One thing his mom and dad *had* been overjoyed about had been getting the chance to be deeply involved in their granddaughter's life. And it seemed yesterday had been no exception—with the trio heading out to Central Park for a walk with their Dalmatian, Jack.

He glanced at his watch, his impatience growing. Lizza was almost a half hour late, and he was supposed to be at work in a few more minutes. He'd been hoping to have a little time to get to know the ropes before jumping right into his morning rounds. But it looked as if that wasn't going to happen.

Out of the corner of his eye he spied a familiar figure at the checkout counter. Only it wasn't Lizza. He groaned out loud.

"What is it, Daddy?"

He pulled his attention back to his daughter's blue eyes. "Nothing. I was just thinking about work."

"Oh. Okay. Do I *have* to go to Mommy's?"

The same question had been repeated for the

past two visits. Clay didn't know what to do about it. Lizza traveled for weeks at a time, visiting European fashion houses in search of ideas for new designs. Molly hadn't spent more than a handful of weekends with her mom in the past year. And Lizza didn't help by being so fastidious about her house and furniture. Molly wasn't even three and a half yet. She needed to be a kid. But he'd learned to keep his mouth shut, as long as his ex didn't do anything to damage their daughter's self-esteem.

So he settled for a response that he hoped was conciliatory. "Mommy would be sad if you didn't."

"I know." Said with a sigh that made his gut clench.

If someone had told him four years ago that after his breakup with Tessa he'd have rebound sex that would result in a pregnancy and marriage, he'd have said that person was out of their gourd. And yet here he was. Only he was crazy about his daughter. So were his parents. It made all the crap he'd put up with from Lizza bearable.

He looked back toward the checkout area just

as Tessa turned around, scanning the place for a spot to sit. It was breakfast time and the place was packed with medical personnel, all scarfing down a quick bite before facing a new day.

Her glance skidded past his and then stopped for a long second, her green eyes closing for a brief instant before reopening and sliding back his way again. She gave him a quick nod and then kept looking for someplace to sit.

Only there wasn't any.

Come on, Lizza. Hurry up.

In the meantime, he couldn't leave Tessa standing there, so he motioned her over. He could have sworn her mouth gave a pained grimace before she moved in their direction. He had no doubt if there had been any other person in the place that she knew, she would have gone to sit with them instead.

He was her last choice.

Well, some things never changed.

She set her tray next to Molly's, her brows coming together slightly, although she didn't ask the question he knew had to be swirling around her head.

His daughter had no such inhibitions. "I'm Molly. Who are you?"

Tessa blinked. "I'm Dr. Camara. How are you?"

"I'm waiting on my mommy."

His stomach tightened again. Left with no other choice, he made the introductions. "Tessa, this is my daughter."

"Is she your friend?" Molly asked.

"An old friend, yes." He looked at Tessa and dared her to correct him. She didn't, dropping into the chair across from him instead.

"That's right. Your dad and I knew each other a long time ago when we were both in school."

"Oh. Did you know Mommy, too?"

Tessa's teeth came down on her lower lip for a minute. "No. I didn't. Is your mom a doctor?"

"No, she makes pretty dresses and fancy clothes."

Tessa's body language changed, fingers clenching on her tray for a second before finally letting go and picking up her glass of juice. "How lucky for you. You must have all kinds of wonderful outfits."

Only she didn't make it sound as if Molly was

lucky at all. There was an edge of sadness that made him look at her a little bit closer. He didn't voice the question in his head, however. "You look like you're in a hurry."

"I have a Mohs procedure to assist with today."

Interesting.

"Mohs? Are you specializing in plastic surgery?" The famed technique, named after its inventor, was used on skin lesions. Lesions that were normally cancerous.

She took a sip of her drink and then shook her head. "Dermatologic surgery. But I hope to do a fellowship in Mohs."

He'd thought her plans had been to go into craniofacial surgery. "That's quite a jump, isn't it?"

"Things change."

"They absolutely do." He couldn't hold back the sardonic note to his voice.

He and Tessa stared across the table at each other for several seconds as the atmosphere around them began to crackle with tension.

No. It wasn't tension. It was the distinctive clickety-clack of a pair of high heels moving quickly across the space.

"Mommy's coming." His daughter's whispered words had a fatalistic sound to them.

He swiveled around in his chair to find that Lizza was indeed headed their way, her perfectly made-up face a huge contrast to Tessa's unadorned freckles and simple style. Tessa wasn't the only one who'd made a huge leap from one specialty to another. The difference between his two exes could give a psychologist enough material to fill a volume or two.

Lizza stopped beside their table, brows lifting slightly in question, while Tessa looked as if she wanted to drop off the face of the earth.

Join the club, honey.

"Hello, Clayton."

She'd always used his full name, rather than the shortened version. He'd liked it at first, because it had been yet another thing that had unlinked him from Tessa, but after a while her formality had worn thin. As had those stupid air-kisses she insisted on giving to everyone. Even as he thought it, she bent down and made a popping sound beside Molly's cheek that never made contact. Neither did his ex attempt to embrace her daughter.

His molars ground together.

No wonder Molly had such a difficult time bonding with her. His parents were all about hugs and real, down-to-earth kisses.

When he stood, though, Lizza made no effort to lean into his cheek as she normally did. Probably because she was now looking at Tessa.

He wasn't going to get out of introducing them, evidently. Perfect. He glanced at his watch. And now he was five minutes late for his shift. "Lizza, this is an old friend from medical school, Tessa."

Tessa murmured that she was happy to meet her, while his ex did nothing but reach for Molly's hand. "Are you ready to go, sweetie? Mommy has some important phone calls to make."

His hands curled at his sides, although he tried to rein in his temper. "Are you sure you have time for her this weekend? I could always drop her back off at Mom and Dad's place."

"It's my weekend." Said as if Molly were simply one more appointment on an already busy calendar.

His chest ached. Molly didn't even have a suitcase, since his ex had a second wardrobe and toys for their daughter at her house. She would launder Molly's current clothes and return her to him in them. Lizza insisted on keeping their households entirely separate. Shades of Tessa and her unwillingness to accept anything from him.

Maybe the women were more alike than he'd thought.

Clay squatted in front of Molly. "I'll see you Monday morning, chipmunk."

One of Lizza's heels clicked in that way she did when she was annoyed at something. Too damn bad.

His daughter threw her arms around his neck. "Love you, Daddy. Be good."

"Aren't I always?" He tweaked one of her braids.

A second later, Lizza and his daughter were headed toward the hospital entrance. A couple of masculine heads turned toward his ex-wife. She was beautiful, he acknowledged, with long blond hair and a delicate bone structure, although he now saw it as a brittle kind of grace that didn't stand up to pressure.

When he examined his feelings about other men

ogling her, he found he didn't care. He'd stopped caring when she'd accidentally forwarded texts to his phone from another man. Someone in Italy that she evidently met up with whenever she was there, despite having a young daughter at home. All that money on counseling for nothing.

The only thing he was grateful to her for was that she'd signed over primary custody of Molly to him without batting an eyelid, saying that with her schedule it was probably for the best.

He couldn't agree more.

Dropping back in his seat, he noticed that Tessa was studying her bowl of oatmeal as if it were fascinating.

He blew out a breath. "And how has *your* morning been?"

The smile he expected didn't come. Instead, she swirled her spoon through the mixture in her bowl.

"It must be embarrassing to have her meet me."

"It was a little different than introducing two colleagues at a medical conference, I'll give you that."

This time her head came up, eyes flashing,

color seeping into her face. "You could have pretended not to know me."

"Why would I do…?" He frowned. "You think I'm embarrassed by you?"

He glanced at his watch for a third time and found that five minutes late had morphed into fifteen. He didn't have time to hash this out with her right now. Not that it even mattered.

Tessa had always had a chip on her shoulder about money or anything associated with it—that probably extended to Lizza's display of expensive clothing.

It wasn't as if she was poor, her parents did well enough for themselves, even if his grandmother's memorial fund had helped pay for her education. Their parents were good friends—they'd worked together for years. When Tessa's parents had realized they weren't going to be able to help her achieve her dreams, his mom and dad had quietly stepped in to help. They were generous people—it was what they did.

In the past, Clay would have tried to smooth things over with her. Right now, however, he was out of both time and patience.

Standing to his feet, he looked down at her. "I think you've got it backward, sweetheart. You always acted like *you* were the one embarrassed, not me."

"I don't understand."

"I don't suppose you do." Time to leave. But first there was a little itch he just had to scratch. "Before I forget, I saw the *capoeira* studio on the list of businesses involved with the festival."

She nodded. "They're putting on an exhibition to garner interest."

"Are you participating in it?" Why he'd asked that, he had no idea.

This time her answer came even slower. "I am."

"You always were good. I'll have to stop by the studio sometime."

He tried to stop the memory of Tessa's long, lithe movements as she trained in *capoeira* from crowding his head, but it was too late—the memories were too vivid…and too raw.

A tightening sensation in his gut—as well as her less-than-enthusiastic response—told him it was time to get out while the getting was good.

So he cut the conversation short with a quick

wave and a "Have a nice day" thrown in for good measure.

As it was, Tessa was the only one with the slightest chance of that happening. Because, between his first ex and his second, his day was well and truly shot.

The foot connected with her cheek with a sharp smack.

Down Tessa went in a tangle of arms and legs.

Marcos was immediately kneeling beside her. "That wasn't supposed to happen. Where is your head, *moça*?"

Her head was where it had been for the past two days. On Clay and the thought of him showing up at the studio unannounced, maybe even with his daughter in tow. Or, worse, with his gorgeous-enough-to-be-a-model ex-wife. The one who fashioned clothes like the ones she'd been given all those years ago. That would be the worst. She'd felt like a field mouse next to an exotic cat as she'd sat there in the hospital cafeteria. Surely Clay had compared them as well and wondered why the hell he hadn't stuck with his wife. Or wondered what he'd seen in Tessa in the first place.

She shook the thoughts away, angry with herself. She was supposed to be training for the hospital festival. And this was geared to be a demonstration that showed off *capoeira*'s romantic side, from its circle of constantly switching partners to the cartwheels, spins and beating drums that made the martial art both beautiful and different. It was more about skill than combat nowadays, but it still clung to some of its former roots. As she'd found out on several occasions. Today being one of them.

One wrong move—or right move, depending on your perspective—and you could take an opponent down. Just as she'd done when she and Clay had been dating, and she'd sent that invitation asking him to come to the studio.

He'd soon been hooked. In fact, she'd done the *batismo* ceremony on him—a match where a more advanced *capoeirista* took down an inexperienced student, formally inducting him into the studio. She'd even presented him with his white cord—the ranking system used by the sport—helping him tie it around his waist. Memories of sweeping his legs out from under him still haunted her dreams on occasion. As did the memory of leaning over him in victory once he'd been flat on his back. His response had made her shiver. With a single raised brow he'd promised retribution later that night.

And he'd kept that promise. Sweet, sweet retribution that had had her begging for more.

"Tessa?"

She blinked back to the present. "Sorry. I just lost my concentration for a second or two."

"A second or two?" Several Portuguese swearwords accompanied the question as the owner of the studio stared down at her. "It's been more like the entire match." He touched a finger to her still-stinging cheek. "I don't want you bruised up before the festival. It defeats the purpose of emphasizing the workout benefits of *capoeira. Intende?*"

"Yes, I understand. Let's try again."

Marcos helped her up and then motioned for the next person in the circle to join her. "Begin."

The percussion instruments set the rhythm once

again as Tessa concentrated on the ebb and flow that accompanied her current partner, the feinting and parrying looking almost choreographed. Two minutes later, she was standing back in the ring of participants as someone else danced in to take her place. When it was once again her turn she slid forward, only to find herself on the wrong side of a foot for the third or fourth time. Mortified, she crashed to the mat, wondering if Marcos was going to take away her purple and green *cordão* and demote her to a lower level.

He knelt beside her once again. "I think that is enough for today, Tessita."

She grimaced. Marcos only resorted to calling her "little Tessa" when he was upset with her. And he had every right to be. She'd trained with him for years and years. He knew exactly what she was capable of. "I don't know what's wrong with me."

"I do not, either, but when you come back next week, try to make our *capoeira* look a little less…brutal."

Everyone laughed, including Tessa, and the

tension eased as he helped her to her feet. She sighed. "Point taken. I'll work on it."

"Good. The festival will be here before we know it."

She grabbed her towel from on top of her bag and blotted the sweat from her face and neck. "Four weeks. I know. Maybe I'll find a few extra hours this week and come in for a private session."

"I think that would be good, Tessita."

Ugh. Still upset. Well, Marcos wasn't the only one. She was upset at herself. Ever since her encounter with Clay in the cafeteria she'd been on edge. Something about the way his ex had looked at her, the acid in her gaze making Tessa feel like a criminal of some sort, even though she'd done nothing wrong.

Well, it was time to put Clay and his ex—and most especially his cute little daughter—from her mind. Once and for all.

How she was going to do that, though, remained to be seen.

CHAPTER FOUR

HE WAS WATCHING HER.

Tessa had caught a glimpse of movement out of the corner of her eye as she continued to section the diseased skin tissue, teasing it away from healthy cells. The Mohs surgery had been put off for three days due to a cold her patient had developed.

How had Clay found out when she would be operating? Maybe Brian Perry, her attending cutaneous oncologist, had clued him in. But why would he have done that? Clay was an orthopedic surgeon, a whole different realm than cutaneous surgery.

She had already marked the surgical site before proceeding and when she lifted the thin layer of tissue and placed it onto a glass slide, she made sure to match the marks so they would know where to continue cutting if the margins weren't completely clear. Brian glanced down at the site and nodded to the lab assistant. "Once you're ready, let us know."

They would section the tissue sample and stain it, looking for areas that still contained cancer cells. Either Tessa or Brian would then remove more tissue just at the specific location. That way they conserved as much healthy tissue as possible.

"How are you doing, Mandy?" Her patient was lying on her stomach with her head to one side, but was wide-awake. Mohs surgery was generally done under a local anesthetic. The only hard part was that there was quite a bit of waiting involved if the tumor had roots that went deeper than expected.

"I'm okay. How's it coming?"

"We'll know in a few minutes."

The buzzer at her waistband went off, as did Brian's. The lab was ready for them to view the slide.

Tessa was glad to get out from beneath Clay's stare. She still had no idea why he was there.

The results under the microscope showed that

there was still one area that contained tumor cells. Brian marked the graph they'd been charting to match what they saw on the slide.

After shaving off two more layers of skin in that area, they finally got the results they were looking for: clear margins. This wasn't melanoma but a squamous cell tumor on the patient's lower left back. While not as dangerous as the type of cancer that had killed Tessa's mom, it could still grow out of control, dividing and penetrating to other organ systems if not caught in time. Fortunately this patient had a known history of skin cancer and had screened herself on a regular basis.

Sucking down a breath, she peered again at her patient as they got ready to close the surgical site. In a calm voice she explained what they'd done and what to expect, thankful they wouldn't need to do a skin graft. Even as she hoped Clay had gotten bored and left, he probably hadn't. She was still stumped as to his presence. Didn't he have his own patients to attend to?

Maybe he wanted to discuss something with her. Lord, she hoped not. The last thing she

needed after the day she'd had was to do a dis-
section of a different kind. Especially if it involved their shared past. It had been over four
years. There was nothing left to dissect.

"Looks good, Tessa. I think you got everything.
Congratulations."

"Thanks." The praise should have elated her
but she was still on edge over Clay's appearance.

As if hearing her thoughts, Brian glanced up
at the window, evidently noticing what she had
a half hour earlier. "Looks like you had an au-
dience."

What did she say to that? I know? Or act as if
she had no idea who it was.

She chose a different route. "Wonder why."

"Not sure. If you feel up to finishing on your
own, I'll go see if I can help him with something.
Maybe he has a surgery in here afterward and is
scoping out the room. He's new." He paused. "I
think you're well on your way to a fellowship in
Mohs, if that's what you're looking for."

Just beneath the hum of excitement that went
through her at the other man's words lurked a trill
of annoyance. This should have been a moment

of triumph for her. She was so close to finishing up her residency. And now a dark specter of the past had to sweep in and ruin it.

Forget it. You did the surgery. Without any assistance or input, for the very first time. That should be all she was thinking about right now.

But it wasn't. And as Brian headed out the door she bit her lip.

She wasn't thrilled about her attending going up to chitchat with her ex, but it wasn't as if she could say anything in a roomful of other medical staff. So she just gritted her teeth and hoped she'd be able to get through the final part of the surgery.

And she should be proud. Clay had seen she *could* do this on her own. Just as she'd promised herself. She refrained from glancing up and making sure he actually *had* seen her finish. But just barely.

She asked for the suture material, and the surgical nurse handed her the pre-threaded needle. Closing the deeper layers first, she worked her way back up to the surface tissue, stopping from time to time to make sure her patient was doing okay. Fifteen minutes later she was done. Brian hadn't come back, and she couldn't bring herself to sneak a peek at the observation room. Instead, she settled for putting the final piece of tape on the gauze and talking to her patient, giving her care instructions and telling her to come back and see Dr. Perry in a week to have her stitches removed. Then she squeezed her shoulder and said her goodbyes.

Pulling off her surgical loupes and then stripping off her gown and gloves, she dropped everything into the appropriate bins. As if pulled on a string, her head went up, eyes seeking the space above her. It was empty. Clay wasn't there, and neither was Brian. Disappointment sloshed through her, followed by relief. The relief was what she chose to focus on. Maybe Clay really did need to see her attending for something. Which meant he hadn't been there because of her. None of that mattered. What mattered was that she could relax.

She pushed through the door to leave the operating room and pulled the clip from her hair so she could redo it. Except the person who'd been in the suite above her was now just outside the door. Quickly finger-combing her hair and cramming the mass back into the clip, she tried to look nonchalant, although her heart was thumping out a nonsensical rhythm in her chest.

"Where's Brian?"

Stupid question. But it was the only thing she could think of to say at the moment.

"He said he had another patient and left me here to wait for you."

Why would he be waiting for her instead of her attending?

"Any specific reason?"

He turned to face her, propping his shoulder against the wall. His face bore no trace of the sardonic amusement she'd come to expect from him. Instead, it was deadly serious. "I talked to my mom last night."

At that, Tessa tensed. She and Clay's parents had maintained a cordial relationship over the years—and despite how uncomfortable it made her feel that they'd shelled out so much money for her education, she was grateful to them. Even after she and Clay had broken up, she'd still had some contact with them. That was until her mom died. She'd barely been able to hold herself together during that time, much less carry on a coherent conversation with anyone outside work. "Oh?"

His eyes searched her face. "I didn't know your mother passed away, Tessa."

Oh, no. Don't do this. Not right now. Not here. Especially since the anniversary of her death had just barely passed.

A sudden rush of moisture coated her lower lids, forcing her to blink several times to hold the flow at bay. "Yes, she did." Licking her lips, she tried to get away. "I have a couple more patients to see, so if you'll excuse me…"

Before she could move past him, though, he reached out and encircled her wrist, his fingers warm and solid against her icy skin. "I'm sorry, Tess. I had no idea. Is that why you changed your specialty?" He nodded toward the double doors of the operating room.

She decided to cut past all the chatter. "Is it why I went into dermatologic surgery? Yes. I suppose your mom also told you what she died of."

"She did." He let go of her hand and cupped her cheek, stroking his thumb beneath her left eyelid. The compassion in his gaze was so different from the blasé attitude he'd shown in front of his poster in the lobby. Then he'd been all cocky with his confident swagger and veiled references to their past.

Tessa felt a telling hint of moisture beneath his fingertip and gave an inward curse. She hadn't quite banished the tears after all.

Taking a step back, she attempted to break free of his touch. "I decided that the best way to serve her memory was to try to help others like her." She stiffened her spine just a bit. "Is that why you were watching me? Because of your mom?"

"You noticed me." One brow went up.

The swagger was back.

Her lips curved despite herself. There was something about this man that did a number on her even after all these years. Did he really think she would miss seeing him there? "It was kind of hard to avoid seeing you, since you were almost directly in front of me."

Well, not quite. He'd been off to the side, but

she'd gotten used to scanning that observation room, which was used quite a bit by both senior doctors and residents in different stages of their work. So, yeah. She'd spotted him almost right away.

"It seemed the best place to find you. You float around this hospital like a ghost."

A ghost? That was one way of putting it. A ghost on a mission was more like it. She'd caught sight of Clay twice on her floor yesterday and had ducked into a patient's room to avoid being seen by him.

Really mature, Tessa.

"Hospitals keep their residents pretty busy. I'm sure you know that from experience." The doors opened and her patient was wheeled out by one of the male nurses. That old wheeling-patients-out-of-the-hospital-instead-of-letting-them-walk-out-on-their-own-two-feet rule was still alive and well. This was the perfect opportunity to escape. "I need to go."

"I'll walk with you. Wouldn't want you disappearing on me again."

What?

"Was there something else you wanted to discuss?" Other than her personal life, that was. She didn't say it, though, since she wasn't anxious for anyone to know that she and Clay knew each other in any way other than as a pair of colleagues…casual acquaintances. She let the wheelchair move a few more yards ahead before turning to follow it.

Clay fell into step beside her. "Yes. Actually, there is."

Clay wasn't sure why he'd gone to the observation room. Maybe out of a sense of nostalgia or morbid curiosity. Or it could be that after his mother told him about Gloria's death from melanoma, something inside him had needed to tell her he was sorry. Despite all of the ugly stuff that had happened between them at the end of their relationship, he'd never wanted anything bad to happen to her or her family.

Why hadn't his mom said anything earlier? Probably because he'd cut her off anytime she'd mentioned Tessa's name. His parents had never known how angry he'd been that she'd thrown his graduation gift back in his face—because he'd never told them. Still, they'd quickly learned she was a touchy subject, one best avoided altogether. The only reason they'd found out that Tessa was at West Manhattan Saints was because of Molly—who'd mentioned the pretty lady that had sat with them at breakfast.

They'd been all ears, probably thinking he was dating again.

Hardly. He was done with marriage, with dating…with women in general.

Then Tessa's name had come up. And the news of Gloria's death had been the first thing out of his mother's mouth.

Regret for all he'd said and done streamed through him. It had grown until the weight of needing to offer his condolences had gotten too heavy. Which was why he was here.

Except as soon as he'd gotten the words out of his mouth he'd felt the need to counter them with a flip comeback seconds later. Why? And why was it only Tessa who brought out that side of him? He didn't do the back-and-forth banter stuff with Lizza—he never had. In fact, he avoided speaking with her as much as possible nowadays.

Tessa was waiting for him to tell her what that other subject he wanted to discuss was. "Remember I asked you about the studio?"

"Studio?" The way she said it, with studied indifference, told him she knew exactly what he was talking about.

"Your *capoeira* studio. I've been thinking about it, and I think Molly might really like to watch one of the training sessions. And if they're practicing for an exhibition, it's the perfect opportunity."

She turned to glance at him, her puzzlement obvious. "You know where it is. It hasn't moved. So why ask me?"

"I wanted to see if you knew when they were practicing. Marcos—if he's still there—probably wouldn't even remember me."

And that was the only reason you wanted to see her, right?

"He'll remember you."

Something about the way she said it made him

slow down just a bit. Tessa, probably not even realizing she was doing it, slowed her pace, as well.

It had been over four years. Surely the studio had had lots of people come and go in that period of time.

"How do you know he will?"

Her glance skittered away. "He may have mentioned you once or twice."

Ah, yes. Clay could see how that might have been awkward for her: explaining why they'd broken off their relationship and why he would no longer be training at the studio.

He could have kept going—he liked the sport. But he'd been so angry at Tessa back then, he hadn't wanted any reminders. Besides, he'd been intent on making a clean break. Seeing her every week at the studio wasn't exactly the best way to do that.

"And I'm sure you gave him nothing but glowing reports."

This time, Tessa stopped completely, an odd look coming over her face. "I never said anything bad about you, Clay." She seemed to hesitate, then continued. "Why don't you let me call him, and I'll get back in touch about a time."

Okay, so she'd just gone from basically telling him to get in contact with them himself to offering to do it for him. What gives?

He decided to press a little harder. "Any particular reason you want to do it?"

She shrugged. "I speak the language. It might be easier for me to explain things."

Somehow he doubted that was it at all. She just wanted to be in control of how much information the school's owner had. It certainly wasn't because of Marcos's English skills, since he spoke it perfectly, although he still had a Brazilian accent. As did Tessa. Just a smidgen...when she got angry or emotional. Clay could still remember some pretty heady times as they'd made love. In the heat of the moment, when she'd been squirming with need, she'd gritted out something in Portuguese. And, man, had it done a number on his control, breaking it into tiny pieces.

The accent had also been there when she'd cut things off between them, the anger and pain in her eyes unmistakable, although he still had no idea what he'd done that had been so terrible. It had only been a bracelet. Lizza would have taken it and run. Except that had all changed after their divorce.

Women.

But now wasn't the time to go into any of that. And going to the studio was probably a bad idea. A really bad idea judging from Tessa's wary expression. But he admired the athleticism of *capoeira* and wanted Molly to experience what he had the first time he'd seen it. Especially since she was going through a phase where she was giving karate chops to everything in sight, including him. He wanted her to see what a real martial art looked like. And to understand that it wasn't about "chopping" people or breaking boards, but about discipline and self-control.

Maybe his daughter could even take lessons, although he had no idea what ages they accepted.

And maybe Clay could even start training again himself. He could use something to help him stay in shape. He could go when Tessa wasn't there. They could still keep their lives completely separate—he'd learned a thing or two from Lizza's insistence on maintaining a his and hers division of households.

His and Tessa's circles never needed to intersect.

Okay, then. He'd done what he'd come to do. Offer his condolences. Now it was time to get the hell out.

He took his wallet from his back pocket and pulled out a business card. "Give me a call when you know something."

Tessa hesitated, and for a moment Clay wondered if she was going to refuse to take it. Then she reached out and plucked it from his fingers, careful not to touch him. At least that's the way Clay perceived it. So he did something about it. He caught her hand, the card trapped between them. He felt her muscles jerk and then relax. "Give my best to your dad, okay?"

"I will. Thanks." Then she tugged free and spun away from him, striding after her patient, who was now long gone. Leaving Clay wondering what the hell he'd been thinking for going after her...for touching her. Because she wasn't the only one who'd reacted. His hand had wanted to linger, his fingers itching to stroke over her palm the way he used to when they were together.

He knew far too well why he'd done it. It had irked him to see her attending standing so close to her while she'd been doing that surgery. And how, when the man had touched her sleeve, she hadn't flinched away from him, as she did with *him*.

He hadn't liked the way it made him feel. Had felt the need to see if she still responded to his touch the way he remembered. She'd responded, all right. He just couldn't tell if she'd been re-pelled by the warm slide of flesh against flesh or if she'd been bothered in a completely differ-ent way.

He could only hope her reaction had been no less disturbing than his had been—a kind of knee-jerk muscle memory that happened with-out conscious thought. He'd been stunned the first time it happened. And the second.

He needed to somehow erase that memory and everything that went with it. Because if he couldn't, he was in big, big trouble.

The first thing to do was make sure he didn't touch her again.

No matter what.

Tessa plopped onto one of the dark dining room chairs in the brownstone house where she lived and put her head down on her arms. Caren Riggs was already home, standing in the kitchen rolling and cutting what looked to be square noodles on the marble island in the center of the space. Right now, though, Tessa was too wrung out to care, even though whatever Caren was cooking smelled divine.

Interacting with Clay was turning out to be even harder than she'd expected. Because when he touched her she quaked. And felt wistful about long-gone days.

She didn't want to yearn for him. That was a million times worse, in her opinion, than simply lusting after that scrumptious bod. Because lust she could explain away—after all, Clay was a hunk of the first order, a vital man who dominated whatever space he happened to stroll past. Even Brian, who was a little older than Clay and just as attractive, with a touch of gray in his sandy-brown hair, didn't make her insides squirm and twist the way her ex did.

And that was bad. Very bad. Because she didn't want to have any kind of reaction at all to him. She was afraid she'd learn something she didn't want to know. That she'd never quite gotten over him.

Sure you did. You broke up with him.

No. She'd broken it off because she'd known they weren't going to be good for each other and had gotten out while the getting was good. That didn't mean it hadn't been painful or that it hadn't ripped her heart from her chest to contemplate never seeing him again.

A few minutes passed as she sat there, and then the table beneath her cheek shifted a bit. Caren had evidently come over and set something down.

"Hey," the other woman said. "You look tired."

"Am." The mumbled word was all she could manage.

"Then eat something. I made chicken and dumplings—classic comfort food. Besides, I have something I need to talk to you about."

Oh, no. This was the second time today someone had used those words.

Tessa looked up to find her friend sitting across from her, and, yes, there was now a shallow, wide-rimmed bowl sitting in front of her. A second bowl sat in front of Caren. The concoction smelled even more heavenly this close to her nose. "What's the occasion?"

"Not really an occasion. I may just not get any Southern cooking for a while, so I thought I'd make some now while I still can."

Caren wasn't from New York, and Tessa found her slow drawl soothing somehow. Even now it seemed to drift through her soul, pushing back the tide of confusion and grief that had gripped her ever since her surprise encounter with Clay in the hospital lobby.

She tilted her head, accepting the spoon the other woman handed across to her. The brownstone, owned by Holly and her family, was decorated in classic dark woods and rich upholstery. It reminded her of what she might find in Clay's parents' home. Wealthy, understated. But for some reason this place didn't make her cringe the way it might have had she not been paying her own way.

"Why wouldn't you get Southern cooking for a while?" She stirred the mixture in her bowl to help cool it.

"That's the thing. I was going to talk to you, Holly and Sam after you all got home. But when you came in first, I thought I'd sound you out about it." Caren paused and eyed her for a second. "Is everything okay?"

"Peachy." She cut into one of the dumplings and blew on it for a second before sliding it into her mouth. Her tastebuds perked right up, a low groan sounding from her throat. She'd never tried honest-to-goodness Southern cuisine before meeting Caren, but she was rapidly becoming addicted. Swallowing it, she smiled. "This stuff is awesome."

"Told you you'd like it. Aren't you glad I forced you to try homemade dumplings after you moved in?"

"I hate to admit it but yes. I've only had the fluffy biscuit kind. These are so good." She waited until Caren had eaten a couple of bites before continuing. "So what's going on?"

Setting her spoon down in her bowl, her friend propped her elbows on the table. "I'm thinking of going on a medical mission."

"What?" Caren had never mentioned leaving the hospital or the brownstone. "Where to?"

"Africa. Cameroon, actually. I just got the go-ahead to start packing."

"Wow, that was fast. What about your fellowship, are you just going to let it go? And what about your unit?"

The house had been divided into four separate units with a shared kitchen, living room and dining room. Over the course of their residency the four roomies had become fast friends. Maybe because they were all young and single, but it was probably also because they shared a common goal of becoming doctors.

She'd just assumed things would stay the way they were for a while. To think of Caren no longer being here…

"That's the thing. I have a cousin who is thinking of coming to West Manhattan Saints and applying for a fellowship." Caren scooped up another bite of dumpling and waved it around for a minute. "She could sublet my unit. All my furniture would stay put. There would just be a new face to go along with it."

A key scraped in the lock just before the front door was pushed open. Sam Napier appeared, carrying a couple of bags, which he switched to the other hand before closing the door again. He glanced at them. "Hi. Am I interrupting something?"

With his longish hair, lean build and the slightest hint of a Scottish accent, Sam could only be described as superhot, but he was also something of an enigma, quiet and intense, rarely sharing anything personal about himself. Maybe it was just a guy trait, but Tessa had a feeling there was more to it than that. Whatever it was, he was definitely the quietest of the housemates.

She shrugged. "You're not. Caren was just…" She glanced at the other woman, wondering if she wanted the medical mission thing kept a secret.

"I was just telling Tessa that I might be leaving for a while. My cousin Kimberlyn—who's also on her way to becoming a doctor—would be able to move in and take over my share of the expenses, if that's okay. I wanted to check with everyone first before giving her a definite answer."

Sam came over to stand by the table. "I don't have a problem with it. I guess it's really up to Holly, though, since she and her folks own the place."

"You're probably right. I'll ask her tonight."

"Is Kimberlyn still in med school?" Sam asked.

"She's a resident, like us. She's just getting ready to apply for a fellowship."

Sam slung a bag over his shoulder. "Sounds like the perfect solution, then."

"I think so, too," Caren said with a smile. "I'm so relieved. I was worried you guys might be upset with me for bailing on you so close to the end of our residency."

Tessa smiled back. "Of course not. I'm excited for you. Besides, you'll be back. And you'll have to send loads of pictures of Cameroon."

"I will." She popped two more spoonfuls into her mouth and then stood. "I'm on call tonight, so I need to jump in the shower really quick. And I'll start packing for the trip."

"Go," Tessa said. "I'll clean this up."

Caren squinched her nose. "It's a mess out there—there's flour everywhere. Are you sure you want to tackle it?"

"Definitely." Besides, it would give her something to think about other than Clay.

"Well, I've got an early surgery in the morning, so I'm going to turn in." With a wave, Sam went up the stairs toward his unit.

"Thanks again. I think you're all really going to love Kimber."

Tessa stood and stacked their bowls. "If she's anything like you, I'm sure we will."

CHAPTER FIVE

"DR. MATTHEWS? YOU'RE needed down in Emergency," one of the nurses at the central station called over to him, phone still to her ear.

Six hours into his shift, Clay had performed two surgeries and done a phone consultation with a doctor from one of the other local hospitals. It had been hectic enough that there'd been whole blocks of time in which he hadn't thought about Tessa once.

Until now.

"What have you got?"

"Looks like they have an elderly gentleman who fell down his front porch steps and broke a leg. Or maybe a hip."

"Tell them I'm on my way." Clay pushed the button on the elevator. The funny thing about fractures in the elderly was that cause and effect were rarely quite as simple as the nurse made it seem. Whether the break caused the fall or the fall caused the break was often up in the air. He'd seen enough spontaneous fractures in his time that he knew brittle bones could suddenly give way under the stress of years' worth of use and abuse.

By the time he got down to the first floor his thoughts were all on his patient, already planning for various scenarios and how he'd deal with each.

One of the attendings stopped him just as he stepped into the hallway where the exam rooms were. "Are you the new orthopedist?"

"Yes, Clay Matthews."

"Anthony Stark. Good to meet you. Your patient is in exam room four. I called in one of the residents as well, once we got a good look at him."

That was odd, since the only orthopedic resident Clay knew of was at dinner. Maybe he'd come back early. "Okay, thanks. Has he been up to Radiology yet?"

"Yes. He just came back. It looks like a displaced break."

Perfect. Displaced meant the two ends of the bone weren't aligned—a more complicated situation to address. Compassion tickled the back of his throat. Another tricky piece of news. He knew of at least one patient in the past month whose heart hadn't been strong enough to do the surgery needed to repair a broken pelvis. He could only hope that was not the case with the current patient.

The sound of someone bellowing came from the exam room where he was headed.

The ER doc gave him a half smile. "All I can say is good luck. Let me know if you need some help in there."

Clay frowned and headed toward the curtained-off area where the sound of voices was growing louder. One female and one male…who sounded none too happy.

Noting that there was no chart in the holder, he swished open enough of the curtain to get through. He stopped in his tracks. Even though her back was turned, the female arguing with his patient wasn't a nurse. It was Tessa. And she was trying her damnedest to pull back the sheet covering the patient, while he held on to the fabric with all his might. Her Brazilian accent was there in all its blazing glory.

Not that it was doing her any good.

"No one is seeing my privates except my doctor!"

"I *am* a doctor, Mr. Phillips. I'm here to look at your leg."

What the hell? Why was Tessa trying to look at his patient's leg? Dr. Stark had said he'd called in another resident, but Clay had assumed it was an orthopedic resident.

If it wasn't for the seriousness of the man's injury, he might have been tempted to just stand back and see how things played out between the two of them, because the Tessa he knew didn't give up once she got going. For anything.

That probably wasn't in the best interest of his patient, though.

He stepped closer. "Anything I can do to help?"

Two heads craned around to look at him. Surprisingly, Tessa's normal irritation at seeing him was nowhere to be seen. Instead, she looked almost relieved.

The patient—Mr. Phillips—yanked harder on

the sheet. "This little lady is trying to get a look at my equipment."

He wasn't sure whether he was more shocked by the "little lady" description or by the fact that a patient was basically calling Tessa a Peeping Tom.

"I'm trying to see his mole."

Ouch.

Wait. Maybe she really did mean mole as in...

"I thought this was my patient. Broken left femur?"

Tessa nodded. "And a suspicious skin lesion on his other leg. Which is why Dr. Stark called me in."

Damn. Of all the rotten luck. So much for the idea that keeping busy could keep him from thinking about her. Because right now his job included the very person he was trying to block out of his mind.

Even more pressing, though, was the need to keep the patient calm. Which meant he just might have to ruffle a few of Tessa's feathers.

Stepping to the other side of the bed, he ignored her for a moment. "How about if I ask Dr.

Camara to step back while I take a look? Would that be better?"

"But—"

He stopped her words with a look. Surprisingly, instead of the dark anger he expected to see on her face she simply nodded, let go of the sheet and took ten steps back until she was against the curtain on the far side of the space.

Glancing at the patient's face and seeing it crumple in relief, he noted a dark bruise where the man had evidently fallen already apparent on his right cheek. As was the pain he'd been holding back. Clay touched the top edge of the sheet. "May I?"

Mr. Phillips released the covering and allowed Clay to pull it down. He edged the gown up as far as he could without totally exposing the man. The area just above his left knee was obviously broken, the frail-looking limb bent at a five-degree angle. And at the top of his other thigh was a dark mark about the size of a quarter.

Irregular edges. Mottled coloring that looked like the boiling up of a tar pit.

Tessa was the expert when it came to skin conditions, but Clay knew enough to bet this was exactly what she thought it might be. Melanoma. The deadliest form of skin cancer. And the most likely to have spread. Whether it had metastasized to his bones and caused the femur to break was something they wouldn't be able to determine without more tests. Regardless, both conditions needed immediate treatment. The break was the most urgent, but the size of the growth on his other leg was also worrisome.

He glanced up at her and gave a nod. "He does have a lesion." He added a quick description, leaving out the actual word.

"I need to see it to be sure."

Mr. Phillips started to reach for the sheet again, but Clay stopped him with a hand to the shoulder. He glanced back up at Tessa. "Could you leave us alone for a moment?"

Even with her red hair pulled back in a clip and twin smudges of exhaustion beneath her deep green eyes, Tessa was beautiful. Probably even more so now than she'd been back in medical school. There was an iron determination that hadn't been there when they'd been together.

Or maybe it had been and he'd simply been too busy—and too entranced by her porcelain skin and vibrant personality—to notice.

But he saw it now, and so he added, "Please? Trust me on this."

Without another word, she ducked beneath the fabric of the privacy screen rather than pulling it to the side.

He turned back to his patient. "Mr. Phillips, Dr. Camara is a professional."

"Still. My wife has been the only woman to see me naked in all these years."

"You've never had a female doctor?"

The man shook his head. The pain had to be excruciating, but evidently the thought of having Tessa see him was even more uncomfortable than his injuries. Clay could always call in another dermatologist—a male one—and risk bringing Tessa's wrath down on his head. But that wasn't fair, either. Tessa was a doctor, and to send her away just because she was a woman made something stick in the lower regions of his gut. So he came up with another solution instead.

"How about if we do this? We'll keep your hospital gown where it is, and I'll cover you with the sheet like this." Clay arranged the folds so that it draped over his waist and created a little "U" of exposed skin. Only the skin lesion was visible. Nothing else. They'd have to examine the rest of him to see if there were any other suspicious areas but they could do that while he was under anesthesia for his leg, if tests showed he was strong enough to even have the operation.

The head of the bed had been cranked up so that Mr. Phillips could see what Clay was doing, and the man visibly relaxed. "I guess that would be okay. But don't let her pull it any farther."

Clay gave him a grave nod. "You have my word."

"Well, okay, then."

"Tessa? Could you step back in here?"

The man turned his head sharply. "I have a daughter named Tessa."

"Well, see there? That must be a sign."

Tessa came over to stand by the bed. "Did I hear you right? You have a Tessa at home?"

"Well, not at home. She'll be forty-nine next

week. Lives in Montana with her husband and three horses."

"Do you have any other family members you want us to call?"

Even as she spoke, her eyes were already on the skin lesion, and Clay could see her mentally sizing it up in her head.

"My wife's been gone for ten years and my two kids—Tessa and Jeremy—live a long way away."

Clay's gut tightened. Maybe Mr. Phillips should think about moving closer to them. But that wasn't up to him. It was up to his family. "Did you give the front desk a way to reach either of them?"

"Yes."

Tessa rounded the exam table until she stood across from Clay, although she didn't look directly at him. Instead, she kept her gaze on their patient. "Thank you for letting me see the spot. We'll need to take that off, maybe even while Dr. Matthews fixes your leg. Would that be all right?"

"I s'pose so. As long as you keep your eyes where they're supposed to be, young lady."

Tessa smiled. "Absolutely. I give you my word."

The man's head fell back onto the pillow, the

pain lines deepening. "Then what d'you say we get this show on the road."

An hour later—with an EKG and bloodwork confirming that Mr. Phillips had the constitution of an ox, even if he had the bones of the eighty-year-old man he was—Tessa shared an operating room with Clay for the very first time.

And the very last time, if she had her way. Her hands might not be shaking, but the rest of her certainly was as Clay stood across from her, working on the broken femur as she excised the skin tumor on the man's other leg. "It's not as deep as it could be," she said, unable to prevent herself from talking as she worked, something she'd always done. No one had seemed to mind it in the past. And Clay didn't seem to mind it now.

But for his part he'd been mostly silent as he worked on drilling holes for the pins that would hold the ends of the patient's bone together and allow it to heal.

Once she'd gotten clear margins, Mr. Phillips would have to undergo a PET scan to see if the cancer had spread. The tumor was large enough to make her uneasy, but things like this had surprised her before. She could only hope for the same good outcome. She glanced up. "How does his other leg look?"

Clay paused for a minute, before meeting her gaze. "I think he's got a good shot, if he's careful."

Keeping true to their word, Clay had made sure that Mr. Phillips's private parts were covered at all times, even though the man would never know the difference. And it made something inside her warm to know that Clay cared about his patient's dignity.

He was a good man. Even if he wasn't the right one for her.

And he wasn't. She'd done a lot of thinking over the past four years about her actions. Her temper—or maybe it was her pride—had gotten the best of her, and she'd ended their relationship in the worst possible way, mailing his gift back to him and basically telling him to get lost.

Yes, maybe someday she would find a way to apologize for that. She wasn't sure when or how, but now that they were working together, surely it was a sign that Fate was giving her an opportunity to make things right. Maybe they could at least become colleagues, even if they could never be friends.

She screwed up her courage, finding it took a lot more cranks of the handle than she'd expected. But she finally took a deep breath and succeeded in opening her mouth. "Do you want to go grab something to eat once we're finished? Unless you've already had dinner."

He eyed her for a second as if not completely trusting her motives. "Where did this come from?"

"If you'd rather not..."

Okay, now she felt like an idiot, but it wasn't as if she could withdraw her invitation.

"Tessa, Tessa..." He clucked his tongue. "I didn't say that."

So what was he saying? That he wanted to go after all?

Before she could ask, he went on, "Molly's staying at my folks' house tonight, in fact. So dinner it is." He put his head down and went back to work as if that was that.

The reminder of his daughter brought home the fact that Clay had a child with another woman. A supermodel, from the looks of his ex. What had happened between them, anyway?

Maybe he'd tried to buy her one too many gifts. Except the former Mrs. Matthews didn't look like the type who would have any trouble accepting gifts or anything else from him.

No, that was just her. Stupid, prideful Tessa, who just had to do everything on her own. She'd come to terms with Clay's parents and had come to appreciate everything they'd done for her. So why couldn't she do the same with their son?

Because she'd wanted to be his equal. Had wanted so badly to know that she could live and survive and thrive on her own, as her parents had done after moving to the United States. That she was every bit as smart as they'd been.

And then Clay had come along with his easy charm and old-fashioned attitude that said it was okay for him to want to take care of her…when she had still been learning how to take care of herself.

Was it his fault that he'd been born into a wealthy family?

No. But it wasn't her fault that she'd been

born into a family who'd had to work hard for every single thing they had, either. And Tessa had wanted to prove that she was cut from the same cloth. That she could work just as hard and achieve just as much as they had. All on her own.

It wasn't rational. She would be the first to admit it. But it was what it was.

She finished up the sectioning of the tumor and dropped the last piece into the collection tray to be taken to Pathology. "How are you getting on?"

"Almost done." He glanced over at her surgical site to find her putting in the sutures. "I'm probably fifteen minutes behind you, if you want to go get cleaned up."

"Do you mind if I watch?" She smiled. "After all, you got to watch me a few days ago."

She wondered if he'd even remember what she was referring to, when he'd stood on that observation deck and made her feel so nervous. She'd started out today as a bundle of nerves as well, but had calmed down once she'd realized he had been just as engrossed in his surgery as she'd been in hers. It had felt almost good to be working side by side with him.

No. Not good. Just not crazy scary, as she'd ex-pected it to be. Maybe even like the equals she'd wanted to be all those years ago.

It gave her more hope that they'd be able to come to some sort of accord, since it was in-evitable that they'd see each other from time to time around the hospital, just as they had today in the ER.

So maybe she wouldn't have to avoid him, as she'd thought she would. Maybe she could just smile and walk on by when she happened to see him, instead of ducking into a room and hiding, as she'd resorted to a few days ago.

He smiled back at her, giving her a jolt when his teeth flashed that slow sexy smile she'd once loved so much. "I don't mind at all, Dr. Camara. By all means…watch me."

A wave of heat washed over her at the words. Because she could remember a time he'd said just that. Only he hadn't been operating at the time. No, he'd been lifting her hips, getting ready to…

God! She physically shook her head, trying to rid it of the images that were now spiraling out of control. How he'd wanted her to watch as he sank into her. Slowly. Deeply.

And she had.

She finished her last stitch and tied it. Then had the nurse cut the suture before dropping her needle into the discard tray, her thoughts in a tizzy.

So…she could just grin and give Clay a happy wave whenever she saw him? Evidently not. He'd just shot that idea to hell.

She took a step back from the table, wanting nothing more than to flee the room. But to do that would look funny after everyone in the surgical suite had heard her ask to watch him complete his surgery. And they'd also heard her ask him out to dinner.

More heat poured through her, pushing blood into her head and making it pound with embarrassment. What had she been thinking? She'd wanted to set the record straight—apologize—but there had to have been a better way to do it than going out to eat with him.

Too late to do anything about it now.

And he probably hadn't even meant his words

the way she'd taken them. He'd just been giving her permission to observe him.

Watch me.

Oh, hell. There it was again.

Think about something else, Tessa.

She focused on his hands, watching those long nimble fingers as they worked on Mr. Phillips's leg. Fingers she could remember running over her in passion, drawing forth reactions she hadn't known she was capable of.

Make this about his job. Not about what you once meant to each other.

She looked at him with new eyes. And what she saw impressed her. He was good at what he did. Confident. Unerring. Just as she hoped to be one day.

If she could just fix herself on those kinds of thoughts, she would be able to get through dinner, and he'd be none the wiser about anything. Like how she still turned to mush just looking at him.

Please, no. Just get through tonight.

Once they were done eating, she would slide back into her normal routine and forget this surgery—with all its terrible revelations—had ever happened.

CHAPTER SIX

"So you're going for a fellowship in Mohs?"

They were sitting in a small restaurant around the corner from the hospital two hours after completing the surgery on Mr. Phillips. Tessa had ordered some scans to make sure the tumor had not metastasized past the site on his leg.

She'd acted strangely at the end of the surgery, though, and Clay had wondered if she was going to back out of dinner. And maybe she should have. Or he should have. It didn't feel half-bad, sitting across from her. Some of the bitterness and resentment he'd had toward her seemed to have leached away over the years.

"Yes, I was planning on applying in the fall, hoping to get an early start."

The waiter interrupted, bringing their wine and taking their orders. When he left again, Clay leaned forward. "I know Dr. Wesley, head of

Oncology. We're friends, actually. I could put in a good word for you."

There was silence at the table for about five seconds. Then Tessa's face turned pink. But it wasn't the soft color that had infused her skin in the operating room, filling him with a heat that had threatened to make itself known to everyone in the vicinity. No, this was a very different kind of red.

She was angry. At least he thought she was.

"Do you think I can't get the fellowship on my own?"

What the hell?

"I just thought since I knew Josiah, I could—"

"Take care of it for me. Help me out."

"Is there a problem with one doctor helping another?"

It was what doctors did all the time. Part of the politics of a hospital, whether he liked it or not. There were a lot more residents than there were fellowship slots. Most people he knew would welcome anything that gave them an edge.

"I don't need any favors, Clay. Or gifts. Or scholarships. Not anymore."

The soft words were said with such quiet conviction that they took him aback. They'd had many arguments about his gift-giving over the course of their relationship, but had their problems extended even further than what he'd thought? "Are you talking about my parents? Was that what our breakup was about…them helping you with a few expenses?"

And there it was. The bitterness he'd felt standing in front of the door of her dorm room was back with a vengeance. He should have known they couldn't have a meal together without getting into some kind of argument. The woman had a chip on her shoulder the size of Mount Everest.

"A few expenses? *Meu Deus!* It was more like my whole education." Her voice rose enough that a couple of people at nearby tables glanced their way. She closed her eyes, her chest rising and falling as she took a deep breath and let it out. "Look at it from my perspective. I thought I had earned that scholarship. I worked hard in college and applied for every financial aid opportunity under the sun. And then to find out that my scholarship had nothing to do with merit or anything else I'd done…"

His stomach tightened. "Why didn't you say anything while we were together?"

"Because I didn't know where the money came from. Not until the day of my graduation." She toyed with her fork, eyes not meeting his.

"You didn't know until…"

Everything fell into place in an instant: why she'd thrown their relationship away with a haughty look of disdain, why she hadn't wanted to talk about anything.

But it was only money.

"No, and you went out with me and never said a single word about it the whole time we were together." Her eyes did come up this time. "I felt so humiliated. My rich boyfriend's parents paid my way through one of the best medical schools in the country. Only no one saw fit to tell me."

When she put it that way, he could see why she'd been so upset that day. But his parents had certainly felt as if she'd deserved the scholarship—had seen it as an investment in the future. Yes, they had a soft spot for Tessa's folks—they were good friends, in fact—but they weren't the kind of people who threw money at a cause they didn't believe was worthy. They'd expected Clay to work just as hard as they did. And Tessa *had* made stellar grades. Better than his, even.

His anger faded. He reached across the table, touching her face. "My parents may have paid the tuition, but you're the one who earned that degree, Tess, not them. I know how many hours you put in studying. And if their scholarship hadn't paid your way, any other awards agency would have been happy to step up to fill in any gaps. Is it so terrible that it was my mom and dad who happened to set it up?"

Her gaze held his for a long second. "I don't know what to think. My parents didn't know about it, either. Wouldn't it have been easier if they had just told us about everything up front?"

"They probably thought your parents would refuse the money if they knew who it came from. They're proud. Very much like a certain young doctor I know." He took his hand away and sat back.

A small smile played about her lips. "I'm just a little proud."

"Oh, Tessa, if that's your definition of *a little…*" He sighed, then fixed her with a look. "You're going to be a damn good doctor. You already are, in fact. I saw you operate on Mr. Phillips's leg."

He hesitated about saying the next thing that came to his mind, but went ahead. "Your mother would be proud of all you've accomplished. And I know your dad is. Mom says he talks nonstop about you."

Tessa's eyes turned soft and moist, the green glittering like meadow grass covered with dew.

"Thank you." The words came out a shattered whisper. "My dad and I miss her more than words can say."

Suddenly his focus slid lower. To the pink lips that had once parted beneath his own. He wanted to part them again…to use his mouth to chase away the pain and grief he heard in her voice.

As if she heard his thoughts, something simmered in the air between them. An electric current that seemed to draw them closer and closer.

If not for the fact that there was a table and

plates between them, he might have leaned across and kissed her right then and there—to see if the experience was as heady as he remembered.

But there *was* a table…along with a whole lot of baggage. So he picked up his fork and speared one of the meatballs on his plate of spaghetti instead. Just because she'd confessed the reasons why she'd broken things off with him, there was no reason to think they could pick up where they left off.

They couldn't.

Too much time had passed. He had a daughter and an ex-wife. He, more than anyone, should know when to leave well enough alone.

Tessa took a bite of her salad, her gaze now traveling around the room. Time to steer the conversation toward something a little more superficial.

"How is Marcos and everyone over at the studio?"

She smiled. "Still as ornery as ever. They're excited about the exhibition." She paused. "Which reminds me, I totally forgot to call him and ask which day would be best."

"Better sooner than later. Molly saw a movie a few weeks ago about a kid who learns to do all kinds of fancy karate moves. She's been going on about it nonstop. *Capoeira* isn't karate, but I think it would seem like it to her."

"I'm sure Marcos wouldn't mind her coming in. I'll try to ask him sometime tomorrow morning." Tessa's lips pursed for a second. "I'm sorry about your divorce."

The shift back to personal subjects took him by surprise, hitting a little too close to home. "Long-term relationships don't suit me, evidently."

She laughed. "You and me both. Your daughter is beautiful, though, so something good came out of it."

Yes, it had.

"She's my life."

Those simple words contained more truth than he'd handed to anyone in ages. They cut to the heart of who he was now, barreling past the flip replies that seemed to come far too easily these days.

He could only hope he and Lizza had spared Molly most of the ugliness that had gone along with their breakup. Those last few months hadn't been pleasant ones. Thankfully Molly had been too young to understand what the fights and arguments had been about back then—unlike now. He did his best, but he still got a sick feeling in the pit of his stomach whenever it was Lizza's turn to have her for the weekend.

He wouldn't put his daughter into a volatile situation like that marriage ever again. Remaining unattached was the best way to guarantee he didn't. Which meant no kissing of spunky redheads was allowed. Unless it was a single night of summer madness that lasted no longer than that.

Now that he'd settled that he could lean back and enjoy himself.

They ate for the next fifteen minutes, the silence broken only by comments about the food and how good it was. The tension that had filled the operating room and their initial meeting seemed to have faded away. Instead, it felt more like those periods of quiet companionship they'd once shared.

Only this wasn't four years ago. It was now.

And where he'd once walked with confidence, he now needed to tread with care. For Molly's sake.

And his own.

Tessa's hand slid over his. "Hey. Thank you for understanding. About what happened all those years ago."

Clay wasn't sure he'd call it understanding in the sense that she meant it. Instead, maybe it was an acknowledgment that mistakes had been made on both their parts.

It wasn't a new day exactly. But the warmth of her skin against his made him think about that single night of summer madness idea he'd had moments earlier. And how he might just like to experience a night like that.

Not smart, Clay.

That didn't stop him from turning his hand so that his palm was facing up and catching her fingers in his.

And then, opening himself to what could be madness itself, he lifted her hand and kissed it.

Shock went through Tessa's system at the firm press of his lips against her skin. Memories old and new swirled through her head and her eyes locked with his as he slowly lowered her hand back to the table. But he didn't let go.

His plate was empty. So was hers.

"Do you want dessert, Tessa?"

She did. Only it was the forbidden kind that she'd enjoy for a little while and then regret the moment she swallowed the last little bite.

She shook her head, still unable to look away.

Not bothering to ask for the check, Clay released her long enough to throw a couple of bills on the table and then stood, hand outstretched.

Her tummy began to twist and turn, half in anticipation, half in fear of what she might say or do.

She gripped his fingers and let him haul her out of her seat in a way that felt like old times— when neither of them had been able to wait for what came next.

Only Tessa no longer knew what that was.

He towed her through the restaurant, nodding at the hostess, who wished them good-night. Then they were outside in the balmy New York air and her back was against the rough adobe finish of the restaurant.

With Clay standing in front of her. Inside her personal space.

He was so close, and when his thumb swept over the back of her hand she jumped.

"Scared?"

Yes. But she knew when to lie. "Not at all. Should I be?"

His fingers gripped even tighter and he gave a slow, knowing smile. "Absolutely."

"Why is that?" Okay, now she was not only scared, she was dying for him to come a little closer, everything inside her coiling in readiness.

And desire.

Another couple went by them on their way to the front entrance of the restaurant, glancing quickly at them and then away again as if afraid of intruding on an intimate moment.

And they were.

Clay must have felt it, too, because he leaned next to her ear. "Exactly how soon do you need to be home, Tessa?"

Her stomach dropped to her feet. Was he asking if she had to be home, period? Because she had no idea what she was going to say if he asked her to spend the night with him.

Um... Okay, think this through for a minute.

He probably didn't mean what she thought he did. It had to be something else. Something different, and she was being stupid and naive.

Except he was still stroking his thumb over her skin with featherlight sweeps that were driving her crazy. And his breath was still warm against the side of her face.

She bit her lip, struggling against the need to close her eyes and just go with the flow. If he did mean what she thought he meant…would she say yes?

Yes.

"I don't have to be home right away. Why?"

How was that for prevaricating? She gave herself a high five for quick thinking.

"It's a beautiful night. I thought we might start with a walk in the park."

Start with?

Her stomach dropped a little lower. Central Park was one place they'd gone when they'd been

dating. To either walk or study…or find a secluded spot.

They'd been kids back then, though.

So thirty-year-olds didn't make out?

He doesn't want to make out with you, Tessa.
Get real!

"Do you go to the park a lot these days?"

"Sometimes. It's a good place to clear my head
after surgery."

Had he gone there after she'd broken things off
with him—walked around all by himself? Somehow that thought made her heart ache. But he'd
never called again after that scene at her dorm,
or even acted as if it had been a big shock.

They'd been fighting on and off for months before that. It had been inevitable that things would
eventually come to a head. If he'd just heard the
cry of her heart back then, maybe the end of the
relationship wouldn't have been so bitter. They
could have parted as friends and gone their separate ways with nothing but fond memories of
their time together.

But, of course, that's not what had happened.
And she couldn't take back what she'd said to

him, even if she wanted to. She still felt justified in breaking things off, in some ways.

She hadn't wanted Clay's gifts or to have him fix things or take care of her. She'd just wanted his love and respect. He'd never been able to understand that. And maybe he still didn't, judging from his offer to put in a good word for her with Dr. Wesley.

Enough, Tessa. Let it go.

One thing she did want to do was go for that walk he'd suggested. Just to put to rest any animosity between them. Although she definitely wasn't sensing any from his side right now.

So she gave his hand a quick squeeze. "The park sounds good."

Twenty minutes later they were looking over the pond as a couple of runners glided past on silent feet. "I remember when I was a teenager," Tessa said, "Mom told me to stay out of the park at night. Things sure have changed over the years."

"My folks were the same way. In fact, I doubt my mother would come here after dark even now unless she had a police escort, and even then it's iffy." He gave a low chuckle. "I probably won't admit I came here, even now."

Clay probably wouldn't admit it to anyone, actually. Especially his mom, who'd been stunned by the abrupt end of their relationship, although Clay had broken it to her in a completely different way, telling her that the decision had been mutual. There'd been no reason to poison his folks' attitude toward her, and at the time he'd had no idea that his parents' scholarship had had anything to do with how Tessa saw him.

Evidently it had.

He was doubly glad he'd handled it the way he had with them. They'd be hurt. Devastated, actually, if they thought they'd had anything to do with her dumping him.

He wished she'd said something. Anything. Maybe they could have worked it out.

No, they couldn't have. If not because of Tessa, because of him. He'd failed at two relationships. There was no reason to think he'd be successful at a third. He had Molly to think about should things get messy.

And they always got messy. Especially when

there was lust pumping through his veins that was as strong as it had ever been.

A police officer came walking by, pausing to glance their way as if mentally assessing the situation. Clay nodded at him and the cop returned the gesture, continuing on his way.

"That's why things are so much better," she murmured. "And it's been cleaned up. It's beautiful here."

It was, with the soft glow of the park lights gleaming off the water…and off Tessa's hair.

Hell, part of the reason he'd suggested coming to the park had been to give himself a chance to think about what he was doing. Kissing her…or anything else was sheer madness.

Yes, it was. The madness of a single summer night.

The words whispered through his skull, a terrible litany that demanded to be heard. Demanded an answer.

Kiss her.

The urge he'd had at the restaurant was back. Stronger than ever.

As if sensing his thoughts, Tessa turned her

face toward him, and her eyes widened. Damn. She always had been able to read him.

And since she could…

He moved a step closer, waiting to see if she'd back away from him. She didn't. So his fingers went to her face, tracing across her right cheekbone, her skin warm and soft, just as it always used to be. He couldn't remember feeling anything softer. Not even Lizza, who always had some kind of cream or ointment smeared over her skin.

Tessa's felt…real. That was the only way he could think to describe it. Flesh and bone, and the softest, silkiest skin known to man.

"Hey." Why he'd said that particular word, he had no idea, except it had always been a kind of signal between them. And it had almost always been followed by a meeting of their lips.

Right on cue, hers curved up at the edges. "Hey, yourself."

That was all it took. His hand went to her nape and drew her closer. It wouldn't be the first time people in the park had seen couples kissing—or more.

And as much as he wanted to just plaster his mouth over hers and grab at everything she'd let him take, he didn't. Instead, he barely touched her. Just a gentle press and release. When her hands went to his shoulders, he repeated the move, his fingers sliding into the hair at the base of her skull as their lips met again. Parted.

As if protesting his teasing, her teeth nipped his bottom lip, sharp enough to sting.

Okay, honey, don't say I didn't try to resist...

This time, when his mouth met hers, all hesitation was gone, and he let her feel the frustration and desire he'd been fighting for the past week. Out it came, spilling over him in a torrent, making him crush her to him as he continued to deepen the kiss.

A quick wolf whistle by another passing jogger almost made him smile. Almost.

Still holding her, he edged her back a little way until they were behind a stand of landscaping that was just tall enough to give them a modicum of privacy. If the cop came back, he'd probably scowl at them and send them on their way.

Clay was willing to risk it. And more. He

crowded her against a tree as his mouth again took possession of hers. Tessa made a small sound at the back of her throat, the hands that had been on his shoulders winding around his neck instead as if she needed to burrow closer. Her breasts flattened against his chest. He ached to reach up and cup them—to see if the weight in his palms was as perfect as it always had been. But he didn't think Tessa wanted to risk a night in jail.

Although there'd been a time when neither of them would have cared. And they hadn't—Tessa coaxing him into the lush greenery of the park and making a few of his deepest fantasies come true.

Just the memory made his flesh leap.

It had been so long.

And when her mouth pulled away from his, he muttered a curse beneath his breath, only to have her laugh and kiss her way up his jaw. "The problem with the park being safer is there are also more people."

"I don't remember that being a problem before."

Her fingers floated down his chest, sliding over his nipples. He sucked in a quick breath.

She'd always been a daredevil at heart—not a hint of shrinking violet in her. Maybe it was the heated Brazilian blood flowing in her veins.

"Tess, I don't think you want to do this."

"Don't I?"

Her hands slid around to the back of his waist and ducked beneath the band of his slacks. She pulled him just a little bit closer, until there was no doubt that she could feel what she did to him. Because it was right there, pulsing against her, wanting nothing more than to shove her clothes aside and take care of business right then and there.

Not a good idea. Not only because of the venue but because if he was going to have her, he damn well wanted it to last more than a few seconds. He wanted to see every last inch of her, feel every secret dip and swell and run his tongue along all those soft curves.

He pulled back, gritting his teeth at the whimper of protest that tempted him to give in and start all over again.

"No," he muttered, his voice coming out rough and dark, even to his own ears. "Not here."

Green eyes blinked up at him. "What?"

Holding her back so he could fully see her face, he gave her a smile that held every lusty imagining he'd ever entertained about her.

"I don't want a quickie in the park. And I damn well don't want it on a night when you have to get up at the crack of dawn." He leaned in until his lips were against her ear, breathing in her scent and letting it slide back out. "It's going to happen at my place, Tessa. And I'm going to keep you there all night long."

CHAPTER SEVEN

CHOP-CHOP-CHOP.

Short little fingers connected with his shoulder in a sharp triplet that had him shaking his head.

Chop-chop-chop. The hatchet-like barrage was repeated for what seemed like the hundredth time.

Clay's mom, standing in the kitchen stirring a pot of pasta, laughed at the bloodcurdling shriek Molly gave for effect.

He gave her a sour look. "Don't encourage her."

Clay had tried a reward system with his daughter, had tried reasoning with her, but nothing seemed to deter her.

The girl spun around on her toes, her hands making various slicing motions that would make any masseuse proud to know her.

"I'm not encouraging her." His mom pointed the wooden spoon at him, eyes crinkling in the corners even though it was obvious she was trying her best not to smile. "Like I said earlier, the sooner you can get her over to that studio, the better."

It had been two days since he and Tessa had kissed in the park, and he'd railed at himself at least a thousand times since. What had he been thinking, promising her a steamy night at his place? He didn't take women there. Ever.

Chop-chop-chop. Molly turned her efforts to one of the bar stools, while Jack laid his head on his paws and did his best to blend into the beige carpet. With his black and white spots, it wasn't working out very well for him.

He patted the side of the chair, inviting his parents' dog over to him. Jack glanced at Molly and then with a low *woof* came over and plopped down on the floor beside him.

"You're not fooling anyone, you old softie," he said, scratching behind the Dalmatian's ears. "She's got you wrapped around her little finger just like the rest of us."

As if to agree, the dog pulled in a deep breath and let it out in a sigh, his brown eyes closing, lids flickering as he fell asleep.

If only he could go to sleep that quickly and easily. But lying in his bed was torture. Especially after telling Tessa he was going to keep her in it all night. Every time he started to drift off, images danced behind his eyelids and he'd jerk back awake.

Chop-chop-chop.

This time it was Clay who was holding back a smile. Just when he got too hung up on all that was wrong with his life, this little girl swooped into his field of vision and turned it all right again.

Getting up from his seat, he went over and caught her up in his arms. "Let's say we go get those little choppers all washed and clean for dinner."

Molly giggled and wrapped her arms around his neck. "When are we going to see *capo... capo...*?" Her tongue struggled over the pronunciation.

"Capoeira." He drew the word out slowly so she could hear it. "And we're going soon. Very soon."

I hope.

With that, he swept her down the hall, knowing

that as soon as dinner was over her little karate chops would start all over again. And continue on the drive home, until she finally fell asleep in her bed.

We're all friends here.

Were they?

Tessa had hoped Clay wouldn't come to the *capoeira* studio when she was there, but Marcos had made a scoffing sound. Right before making his comment about them all being friends.

Besides, he had something to run by her, he'd said. And by Clay.

That filled her with trepidation more than anything.

She pulled up to the studio to see that Clay's car was already in the parking lot, but he wasn't in it. Great. She definitely didn't want Marcos relaying some scheme while she wasn't there to mediate. She'd never told the director of the studio what had happened between her and her ex, and he'd never asked. But surely, since Clay had stopped coming in to train, he'd figured out they were no longer together. At least she hoped he did.

When she pushed through the door to the studio, she saw the man in question immediately. He was there in the middle of a swarm of *capoeiristas* with his daughter. Everything in her relaxed. He'd said he wanted Molly to see a training session, so it hadn't just been a line.

And after that kissing session in the park she'd halfway expected him to show up on her floor and start making plans about that night he'd talked about.

She'd had second thoughts about that. She could only hope his absence meant that he'd reconsidered, as well.

It had been a warm, dark evening, and the park had been beautiful. It had been natural that it would bring up old memories and emotions.

Emotions that had no place in her hectic life right now. She was getting ready to complete her residency and apply for that fellowship. The last thing she needed to do was rekindle a romance that was dead and gone.

Was it?

Of course it was. But she was also a young woman with normal urges. And it had been a very long time since she'd been with a man. Well over a year.

If Clay propositioned her, she couldn't guarantee she'd say no. But it would be with the understanding that it was just about the sex.

S-E-X. Nothing more.

That tick-tick-tick going on inside her chest was not some biological clock warning her time was running out. Her residency took priority. But once that was done she planned on looking into adoption. Or checking into in vitro fertilization, using a sperm donor.

Clay's blue eyes met hers and one side of his mouth tilted up in that crazy sexy smile. Okay, so she'd been staring at him as all those thoughts had gone wriggling through her head—just like a thousand swimmers all headed for the prize. Great. Clay was *not* a potential sperm donor, and she hardly thought he'd be amenable to dumping a sample in a cup and handing it over to some fertility expert.

No, he'd want his donation to be up close and personal.

She shivered for a second before realizing Marcos had said something.

Clay's brow went up, his smile widening.

Caught again! Damn.

She dragged her eyes away from him and found Marcos at the front of the room. "I'm sorry?"

"I said it was good to have Clay back in the studio, Tessita. Do you not think so?"

Tessita. Oh, no. He was already irritated with her.

"Yes. Of course it is." She kept her eyes off Clay and fixed them firmly on Marcos.

"Do you want to show him what you're working on?"

"What?" Oh, no. She hadn't planned on training in front of him. "It can wait. Really. I think he just wanted his daughter to see what *capoeira* is."

"And who better to show it to her than someone who has mastered the sport, *não é*?" Marcos held out his hand. "After all, he has seen you train before. He has trained with you."

I've done more than that, Clay's glance seemed to say.

She wanted to send Marcos a biting reply in

their native tongue, but Clay would know they were talking about him. Or arguing about him. She didn't want him to think his being here bothered her at all.

Even if it did.

Marcos clapped his hands. "Form the circle. And we begin."

The *practicantes* gathered in a loose ring, Clay standing just a bit back, still holding Molly up where she could see.

Tessa hadn't even changed into her *capoeira* gear yet—she'd been running late from the hospital. All those recent night shifts had wreaked havoc on her concentration. She also hadn't expected to be dragged into an impromptu exhibition. So she was in yoga pants and a loose T-shirt.

Something in her wondered exactly what Marcos had up his sleeve.

She moved to join the circle of students, dragging her T-shirt to the side and tying a knot to hold it tight against her waist. The last thing she wanted was for it to ride up in front of everyone when she did some of the flips and twists she'd been practicing.

The studio's tambourine players started things off, snapping out the typical beat of the studio, while the stringed bow added its own unique twist. The rest of the circle joined in, clapping and chanting in time with the beat. Pointing at two of the studio members, Marcos signaled for them to be the first to enter the ring. The men moved forward and began the advances and feints that were typical of the martial art. One of the men fell as he attempted a single twist backflip, but leaped back to his feet.

"Ai caramba, gente. Força!" Marcos waved the man out of the circle and jabbed a finger at another participant, who took his place. The other *capoeirista* didn't miss a beat, just engaged the new guy. Back and forth they went in a perfectly synchronized dance that often came within a foot or two of crashing into the bodies that formed the human cage behind them but not so close as to be a real danger to anyone.

Tessa clapped in time with everyone else, but glanced back at Clay, who stood on the outside of the ring. She'd always stood next to him in days past, translating whenever Marcos had gone on

a tirade about something in Portuguese. He nodded, indicating he got the gist of it, although with
the way the fallen guy had slunk out of the center of the circle it was pretty obvious he'd been
scolded. He shifted his daughter to the other arm
and said something to the girl with a smile. She
then started clapping along with everyone else.

She couldn't hold back her own smile. One
of her earliest memories was of watching her
dad in the ring, doing some of these very same
moves, and the memory of receiving her very
first cord—the *capoeira* equivalent of a belt. It
had been white. She'd rapidly worked her way up
the ranks, although her advancement had slowed
once she'd gone to medical school and had only
been able to come once a week rather than the
usual three that most of the serious participants
trained. The purple and green *cordão* she currently owned signified she could be an appren-
tice instructor if she wanted to.

But she didn't have time to do anything except
practice medicine and come to the studio once
a week.

Marcos treated her as if she were one, though,
being tougher on her than he was on a lot of the

other students. Since she was participating in the exhibition, he had good reason to be. One mistake and the public demonstration would be ruined—and, like most Brazilians, he would see it as a reflection on his teaching abilities. And he would not be pleased.

Marcos motioned for a new player to enter the ring, the flow in and out of the circle seamlessly performed. A few minutes later it was her turn.

Gritting her teeth, she forced her concentration to spiral down to what was contained within the circle, not allowing it to stray as she performed a low bent cartwheel, which moved her to the center of the area. She immediately went into a *cadeira* squat as the other player swung his leg in an arc over her back.

Clay had once said *capoeira* looked like a form of breakdancing. With the sweeping circular movements and spins, she could see why he thought that. But a lot of the moves were contained in other martial arts—they'd just been modified a bit and put to a beat. *Capoeira* had become a kind of art in motion in a lot of studios, rather than outright combat.

She twisted her body and went on her hands,

both legs gliding over the other person's bent head. Keeping the rhythm pulsing in her brain, she swept over and around and circled her opponent, her body constantly in motion, gaining speed as she went.

Her rival matched her move for move until there was nothing but the leaps and vaults and spins that swept her into another realm. Tessa likened it to a trancelike state, except she was aware of everything. Even the small commotion currently going on somewhere outside the circle. Her opponent backed up a few paces, still sweeping and twisting and ducking in time to her moves, but she sensed a change coming. Then he was leaving the ring and another player was entering. Not a *craque*, as she called experienced *capoeiristas*, but a novice.

She dialed down her pace and with a backward twist came face-to-face with her new partner. She faltered, almost falling right onto her head in the middle of a handstand before catching herself.

It was Clay.

What was he doing? And where was his daughter?

Those two thoughts ran through her head before Clay jumped high into the air, one leg sweeping over her as she came out of her handstand. She countered him with a leap of her own, her foot coming within inches of his chest as he spun back and went into a low crouch, one leg going beneath hers as she leaped over it.

Her heart began pounding, her concentration slipping in and out as they continued to parry and evade, advance and retreat. It was as if somewhere inside Clay he'd retained everything he'd been taught. Still a novice, but sure and confident and never giving quarter if she didn't force him to. And she had to. She had to put an end to this or she was going to make a fool of herself in front of everyone. She edged in closer, still twisting and turning and leaning back whenever a foot or hand swished past her. She looked for an opening and found it within seconds. Making it look like an accident, she swept Clay's legs out from under him in the *batizado* move she'd taken him down with all those years ago.

And he did go down, his back hitting the mat with a loud slap that reverberated through the studio. Breathing heavily in the absolute silence that followed—since the drums and other instruments had stopped playing—she stood over him, only vaguely aware that he'd suddenly moved with lightning speed, his legs scissoring hers and jerking them out from under her. She fell right across his chest.

Argh!

She opened her mouth to yell foul, but instead found herself laughing. He'd learned a thing or two since leaving the studio, evidently. Because even though she'd gotten the best of him, he hadn't let that stop him from turning things right back around.

The sound of someone clapping in a slow, rhythmic way broke through everything else.

"This!" It was Marcos, and far from being angry at how she'd stopped the session he seemed delighted. "There is still that same fire between you. You must bring this to the exhibition."

What? Her eyes widened in horror, and she leaped to her feet with a clumsiness she'd never had in the ring before.

No, no, no!

This was Marcos's plan for the big finale he'd talked about?

There was no way in hell she was going up against Clay during that exhibition. She wouldn't have even done it now if she'd known her friend was going to throw him into the ring while she was there.

Clay stood as well, leaning down to her ear. "Did you know about this?"

Well, if Marcos wasn't angry, Clay more than made up for it. Because he was furious.

"No, I did not know." Her voice came out as a hiss that matched his.

Several other players came into the circle and slapped Clay on the back, everyone laughing and talking at the same time, completely unaware of the tension flowing between them.

"What better way to end the exhibition than to have two doctors from West Manhattan Saints enter the *roda* together?" Marcos smiled at both of them. "We will have posters made up with your pictures and—"

"I'm sorry. I can't." Clay's voice cut off the spiel in midstream. His easy charm was nowhere to be seen.

Tessa swallowed hard, trying not to let the pricking sensation in her gut mean anything.

Marcos countered, "But it will be perfect."

Perfect? A perfect disaster maybe.

She shook her head, agreeing with Clay, even as the jabbing in her midsection increased. "It won't work. There's not enough time to practice. The festival is only three weeks away."

"I will train you myself. And it will be a *good* thing if the moves don't look so planned. It will help people see that anyone can train in *capoeira*."

"Sorry. No." Clay headed out of the ring, going to where one of the other members held Molly and taking her.

The little girl, unaware of the tight lines of her father's jaw, brought the side of her hand down on Clay's shoulder with a quick whack. "Fun!"

No, it hadn't been fun. Clay's outright rejection hurt more than she wanted to admit, but he was right. Her nerves were stretched to the breaking point just from being in the practice ring with him. If she had to go up against him in front of thousands of people…

She'd be a wreck.

No, Clay had made the right call. And if she knew him, nothing would change his mind.

Not Marcos…or anyone.

Peter Lloyd was seated behind his desk, writing furiously on a report, when Clay entered the room. He had no idea what the hospital administrator wanted. In fact, he'd only met the man a couple of times. Once when he'd decided to transfer to the hospital to be closer to his apartment and his mom and dad's place. And the other had been when he'd come in to fill out the paperwork. To be suddenly called down to his office made no sense. Unless there was something he still needed to do to finish his file.

"Ah, Dr. Matthews, come in and have a seat. I'll be with you in just a moment." True to his word, the man kept writing while Clay lowered himself into one of the leather chairs that flanked his desk.

Nothing like trying to intimidate your prey.

Only Clay wasn't intimidated. He'd done nothing wrong.

Mr. Lloyd glanced up from his papers and pulled another sheet in front of him. "You've heard about the yearly Health Can Be Fun festival we hold to fund cancer research by now."

Clay immediately tensed. He still hadn't volunteered to do anything. He'd meant to do it this week, but then the *capoeira* session had messed with his head. As had Tessa. She seemed just as anxious to avoid being paired together as he was.

Except in Central Park. She'd certainly seemed willing to be paired in a completely different way when they'd been there.

"If this is about the sign-up sheet, I know I haven't put my name on it yet, but I will. I fully intend to support the campaign."

Tessa's mom came to mind. How great would it be if someday cancer no longer took loved ones from their families?

"Good, good." The man pushed the paper away. "Glad to hear it because a special opportunity has just presented itself."

"It has?" Clay had no idea what the administrator was talking about. But he got the feeling he was about to find out.

"Actually, the opportunity is for you and Dr. Camara. It'll provide great exposure for the hospital."

His gut clenched. Had Tessa actually come back here and said something about the *capoeira* studio? She'd seemed just as against it as he was. Or had that all been an act?

He forced his mouth to say the words. "What exactly does this opportunity entail?"

Mr. Lloyd sat back in his chair. "I hear that you and Dr. Camara used to train together at one of our sponsor's studios."

He heard the words through a buzzing in his skull that was growing louder by the minute. "Are you talking about Traditional Capoeira of Brazil?"

"Yes. So you already know what I'm going to ask."

Clay shook his head. "Not really." Actually, he did, but he was hoping against hope he was wrong.

"The owner of the studio stopped by and made a convincing argument. He said this could be a huge draw to the festival. It would help the studio, and it would help the hospital. A win on both sides." Mr. Lloyd reached behind his desk and pulled out a rolled-up poster board. When he slid the rubber band off the tube of paper Clay's clenched gut tightened even further. It was an old snapshot of him and Tessa at his ceremonial induction, when his first cord had been presented to him.

Tessa's leg was outstretched and poised just behind his knee. It was right before he'd gone down. Only the image had now been blown up to gargantuan proportions.

Hell. He and Tessa looked happy.

Really happy.

Looking at her face, he could remember what they used to be like together.

"I don't think Dr. Camara is going to agree to this. In fact, I'm pretty sure this would not be a good idea."

The administrator frowned. "You're new here, aren't you, Dr. Matthews."

"As of a week ago, yes." That was when he realized he wasn't actually being asked if he would like to participate, he was being told.

"The studio has been one of our sponsors for a

number of years. In fact, their exhibitions always attract quite a crowd." He sent Clay a smile that looked genuine for the most part. "Hell, even my wife went over and took a few lessons from them after seeing it one year. So what do you say?"

There was a pregnant pause while the administrator's eyes remained on his.

What choice did he have?

"I guess I say yes, provided Dr. Camara agrees." Tessa was going to have his hide. "Have you already spoken with her about it?"

"I thought I'd leave that to you. She was already planning on taking part in the exhibition, so this shouldn't be much of a surprise to her."

Oh, it was going to be a surprise, all right. And not a good one. He'd be lucky if he came out of there with his head intact.

"I'll see what I can do."

Great move, Clay.

He sighed. Surely they could work together for five or six hours without killing each other. And it would benefit the hospital and those in need. No big tragedy. They were both adults. They would get through this and come out stronger on the other side, right?

"Oh, and we'll want to get your and Dr. Camara's formal permission to use this poster. We'll put some of them up in the hospital entryway and some other places. It'll help get the word out about one of the highlights of the festival."

Highlights?

It just kept getting worse.

The last thing he wanted was to have a spotlight placed on that picture of him and Tessa together. Not because it was embarrassing or humiliating but because it hit too close to home—was too much of a reminder of what he and Tessa had once meant to each other.

She was going to blow her top when she heard about this. And his parents. They were going to get their hopes up that he and Tessa would get back together. At least his mother would. Of that he had no doubt. He was somehow going to have to figure out a way to nip that in the bud. Because there was no hope. No hope at all.

A single night of summer madness? Well, it

looked as if the exhibition might turn into exactly that.

He left the office and headed for the bank of elevators. Once inside one of them, he punched the button for the third floor and leaned against the wall, waiting for the doors to open. When they did, he was surprised to see Tessa there. From the furrowed brows and flashing green eyes he gathered she was upset with someone. Well, so was he.

As he made to step off the car he found a hand planted flat on his chest, pushing him backward. She moved into the space and pressed all the buttons one by one.

What the...?

The doors closed, and it started moving up—with him and Tessa as its only occupants. She turned toward him. "What is going on? I just got a call from Marcos that you've decided to take part in the *capoeira* exhibition after all."

He tried to wrap his head around her words and failed. He'd only just come out of Lloyd's office. Surely word couldn't have gotten back to her or Marcos this fast.

"Did you already know about this?"

The doors on the next floor opened and, when no one got on the car, closed again. The elevator continued on its course.

"Know about what? That you were going to go to the administrator and ask him to put you into the exhibition?"

"No. That would have been you."

"Me?" Her eyes widened. "Why would you think…? Hardly. I thought you said you didn't want to do it."

"I don't."

"Then who…?"

"Marcos." They both said the name at the same time. Clay's muscles relaxed and he leaned back against the wall of the car. Lloyd had said it was Marcos, but he'd only half believed the man.

The elevator stopped again, the doors opened and then closed once more. He could have gotten off and walked up the two remaining flights of stairs to his floor, but he didn't. "So what are we going to do about it?"

"What can we do? Between Marcos and Peter Lloyd they've got us right where they want us."

He laughed. "And where is that?"

"Putting on a show for anyone who wants to watch."

For some reason a lurid image came to mind, of Tessa again sprawled across his chest. But this time, instead of leaping to her feet, he stopped her, his hand sliding into her hair and angling her head within reach of his mouth.

He swallowed hard, trying to banish the mental picture. It didn't work. So he trickled a bit of gasoline on the spark to make her aware that she was treading on dangerous ground. "Then we'd better make that show worth their while, don't you think?"

This time her face tipped up to look at him. Seeing what was written there, her lips parted and she blinked. "That could be awkward, Clay. Very awkward."

"Could it?"

Clay remembered playing these games with her many times in the past. Suddenly all thoughts of his mother getting her hopes up fled as those memories crept closer to summer madness.

"They have a poster already made up. The one taken at my *batizado*."

"The one where I… And afterward we went to your place and…"

"That's the one."

Two more floors came and went. After the next one they'd be heading back down the way they had come. The doors opened and this time a nurse got into the elevator. He nodded a greeting at the newcomer, who turned to stare at the readout, her head craning to the side, probably wondering why so many floors were lit up.

Tessa's cheeks turned a shade of pink he recognized all too well.

She was the one who'd pressed all those buttons. And he realized he'd squandered his chance to act on their time alone. Except that little camera in the corner—which he hadn't noticed until just now—would have caught them in the act. Good thing someone had interrupted or the poster the administrator hung on the walls might be even more suggestive.

Not the kind of staff behavior Mr. Lloyd would approve of.

There was silence for two floors, then the nurse got off, leaving Tessa and Clay alone once again. Despite the danger, he couldn't resist pressing just a bit harder. "So we'll have to practice," he murmured.

"More than likely." She flushed even more.

Hell, he'd love nothing more than to crowd her against that wall and mash his lips to hers. Instead, he crossed his arms over his chest. Time to cool things down a little. "What day were you planning on going over to the studio?"

The elevator stopped again, and this time Tessa pushed the button to hold the doors open. "This is my floor. But I'll be over there Tuesday at five."

"I'll see you there, then." Three days from now. "To practice."

She stepped off in a hurry, saying nothing more. Soon the doors slid back together and cut her off from view.

What the hell had he just gotten himself into?

This was crazy. Except the anticipation flooding his veins and infiltrating his thoughts said something completely different. That the only crazy thing was thinking about what would happen when the exhibition was over and done.

And when he and Tessa finally went their separate ways. Once and for all.

CHAPTER EIGHT

TESSA'S ATTENDING WAVED to her as he walked past the desk where she was reading through some of the newer protocols on melanoma. It seemed research was showing that the depth of the tumor wasn't always the best predictor of whether or not it would metastasize, rather it depended on the type of melanoma itself. So even very thin tumors could be deadly.

"Do you want to check on your patient this morning?" he called.

"Mr. Phillips?" The elderly gentleman was still recovering from surgery on his broken leg. "Have you gotten the results back on his scan?"

Brian backtracked until he stood in front of her. "I was just going to check the computer to see. We can stop by my office on the way."

"Sounds good."

She followed him down the corridor to where

some of the staff offices were. Once there, he sat behind his desk and she slid into one of the chairs in front of it. Tapping the keys on his computer, he soon pulled up the file and turned the monitor so they could both look.

Flipping through the different slides, he soon got to one that made Tessa lean forward. "Oh, no."

Mr. Phillips's liver had a couple of hot spots on it, as did his lungs. "I see them. We'll need to talk to the patient and then assemble a treatment team."

Tessa's heart contracted. The leg break was now suspect, as well—although it could be coincidental, due to his age. They wouldn't know for sure without a bone scan. And at almost eighty she wasn't sure what kind of intervention his body could handle. If they'd caught the cancer earlier…

Memories of her mom's fight came winging back. It had been a similar case, only her tumor had been deep-seated, roots extending down to the lower levels of the dermis before it had been caught. By then it had been too late. It had spread everywhere.

None of that helped them right now, though. All they could do was come up with a plan.

Brian looked up. "Thoughts? He's officially your patient."

And this was where the weight of responsibility became heavy. It was one thing when you worked under someone and they made the final decisions. Tessa was rapidly coming to a time in her career where she would make those choices. As much as she might wish it were different, to have it any other way would be a cop-out. Brian was basically handing this case to her. She should be ecstatic. Instead, she was swamped by indecision. But she'd better snap out of it or she may as well hang up her scrubs right now. So she stiffened her spine.

"I concur with what you just said. His daughter flew in to see him pretty soon after surgery, and she's got medical power of attorney in the event that anything happens, if I understood her correctly."

The daughter whose name was Tessa. The memories of Mr. Phillips protecting his modesty seemed bittersweet now.

"Good," Brian said. "DNR order?"

The tightness in her chest grew. *DNR... Do Not Resuscitate.* "I don't know. I was hoping the section was all he'd need."

"I'll need you to check on that. Talk to the daughter."

She knew that Brian didn't mean to sound brusque. It was part of remaining objective enough to do what was best for the patient. And she should be grateful that he was guiding her through the necessary steps, because right now her head was spinning. She'd lost other patients, especially when she'd done her trauma rotation. But there was something about this one...

Maybe because she and Clay had worked side by side on him—as if by joining forces they could double their healing power. But there was an inferno raging within Mr. Phillips's body that would take a miracle to put out.

"I'll talk to her."

"I was going to go down with you, but the fewer people in the room when he hears the news, the better." He studied her across the desk. "Are you up to this?"

Was she? This wasn't going to be an easy conversation. And she could probably say the word and Brian would go down in her place and handle everything. She wouldn't ever have to see Mr. Phillips again. But sometimes caring about a patient meant having to relay difficult news and muddling through it the best you could. And if she was ever going to be able to do this job on her own, she was going to have to take the bad with the good. Walking with the patient, working together to make the very best choices, brought its own rewards—even if that reward was in bringing honor and dignity as they made end-of-life care decisions.

But they weren't there yet. The team would meet and come to a joint recommendation. That was, depending on what Mr. Phillips wanted to do.

"I'm up to it." She stood. "I'll let you know what the feeling is from Mr. Phillips and his daughter."

"Call me if you need me." He glanced back at the screen, where those bright spots seemed to glitter an unspoken accusation at her. "And, Tessa, I'm sorry. I didn't expect to see this any more than you did. Sometimes these things just don't follow any pattern."

Maybe they did, though, in this case. The tumor hadn't been all that deep, and she'd gotten down to clean margins. But somehow those cancer cells had ventured outside that dark circle and burrowed deep inside Mr. Phillips's body. She wondered if Clay knew yet.

Probably not. He was an orthopedist. That's where his efforts would be concentrated. No need to even contact him with the news. Besides, he could pull the results up just as easily as she could, if he wanted to.

"Thanks. I'll let you know how things go." With that, she left his office. About halfway down the hallway she stopped and leaned against the wall, drawing a couple of deep breaths and trying to organize her thoughts. No sooner had she done that and gotten on the elevator that her time with Clay in this same space filled her head and made tears spring to her eyes.

The back-and-forth innuendos and laughter seemed crude now.

You're being ridiculous. This is part of being

a doctor. If you can't handle it, you'd better get out now.

Someday she would take a patient's diagnosis in stride, as Brian did. As Clay probably did. But today was not that day. Not with the anniversary of her mother's death still clinging to her thoughts.

The elevator stopped one floor down and opened, leaving her staring at the glare from the brightly waxed linoleum tiles. It took the elevator doors marching back toward each other to make her reach out to stop them. She stepped off and glanced at the board that listed the patients and room numbers. Mr. Phillips was still in room five, down to the left.

When she arrived she heard laughter coming from inside. Giving a quick knock and forcing a spring to her step to avoid looking like a funeral director, she entered the room.

Someone was sitting in a chair next to the head of the bed, a grin on his face that was as big as Mr. Phillips's. Two pairs of eyes swung toward her. But it wasn't the man's daughter who sat there. It was Clay.

He kept smiling, but a subtle shift took place as his eyes met hers. She made her own lips curl, although it took an enormous force of the will to get those muscles to tighten.

She glanced around the room, hoping his daughter might be there. But she wasn't. Just Mr. Phillips and Clay.

"What are you two talking about?" she asked. Her voice was light enough, but it had an artificial timbre to it that reminded her of those sweetener packets she used in her coffee.

Mr. Phillips's eyes crinkled around the corners. "Just comparing notes."

"Guy notes." Clay's gaze never left her face.

He knew. She could see it in the slight movements in the muscle at his cheek, in the firming of his glance.

And it was Clay who provided the opening she needed. "I was telling Mr. Phillips his break is healing just the way we like to see. Do you have news on that spot you removed?" He stood and motioned her to take the chair so she could be closer.

"I do. Do you want your daughter to be here?"

Just like that, the crinkles disappeared, dying a terrible death. "That bad, huh?"

Tessa could have taken the chart and studied it as if there was something important written there and avoided meeting Mr. Phillips's gaze altogether, but she wouldn't do that to him. She owed it to him to be direct and honest, without taking away all hope. "Your scan showed some areas that we need to look into."

"Where?"

"Your liver. Your lungs."

The man's breath exited in a soft sigh. "Cancer?"

"We need to do so some more—"

"Tessa." That single word came from Clay.

Mr. Phillips looked from one to the other. "I've been around the block a couple of times. Something's eventually going to get me. Why not this? I've outlived most of my friends. My brothers and sisters. My wife. So just give it to me straight."

Swallowing, she nodded. "Yes. We're pretty sure it's cancer that has spread from your leg. We're going to get a treatment team together and see what we come up with."

He looked at her for a minute or two. "You do your talking. But if it doesn't look like an easy fix, I'm going to have to turn you down. I can't do that to my daughter and son, and she's traveled a long way to see me already. At least I'll have time to say my goodbyes."

Mr. Phillips's wife had died almost ten years ago of a massive stroke. She'd been dead before she'd hit the ground.

Tessa wasn't sure which was worse for those who were left behind. Watching your loved one wither away before your eyes or having them snatched in an instant.

"Do you want me to speak with your daughter?"

"She'll probably want to talk to you herself, but I'd rather break the news to her." Mr. Phillips reached out and gave Tessa's hand a squeeze. "It's okay, honey. I've been ready for a while now."

She wrapped her fingers around his for a few seconds. "As soon as I know something more, I'll let you know."

"I know you will." Rheumy eyes moistened.

"I don't mind telling you, I miss my wife. I'll be glad to see her."

Clay's hand landed on her shoulder, whether in support of her or Mr. Phillips she had no idea. But she was glad he was there.

"Don't make your reservations just yet, Mr. Phillips." If she could will someone's cancer to go up in a puff of smoke, this would be the person she did it for. But she couldn't.

"Can I talk to you outside, Dr. Camara?" Clay's low voice made her nod.

But before she got up... "Is there anything you need? How is your pain level?"

"I think it's better than yours right now." Her patient let go of her hand and gave her a smile. "Don't be sad for me, honey. It's going to be okay."

She gave one more nod, unsure she could force another word from her mouth, then stood to her feet, following Clay out of the room.

Once there, he turned to face her. "You okay?"

What was it with male doctors asking her if she was all right? She was a professional, just as they were. Her head went up, along with her temper. "Fine. Why?"

He made a tsking sound with his tongue. "You wouldn't be human if it didn't get to you. Especially with some patients."

"Brian seemed just fine." Her face felt carved out of stone.

A frown appeared on his face. "You saw him?"

"Um, yes. He's my attending. We just finished discussing this particular case."

"That's not what I meant. Did he mention them?"

"Them who? I don't understand." Sadness morphed into confusion.

"You don't know about the jars."

She blinked. "Jars?"

Taking her elbow, he led her a few feet away from Mr. Phillips's door. "It seems some collection jars have been set up at some of the nurses' stations."

Okay, now she was getting irritated. "They always put up jars before the festival. The staff contributes to whatever charity the hospital has chosen this year." It seemed a little weird for him to have pulled her out of a patient's room to tell her that. Unless he was trying to spare her feelings.

"Yeah, I don't think these are the kinds of jars they normally have out."

Glancing across the space, she saw the nurses' station was empty of personnel, but it did indeed have a jar. In fact, there were a pair of them. That was strange. Why would they need two?

She walked toward the containers and squinted at the writing on the first one. Someone's name... Her thoughts fell off abruptly.

No, not someone's name. *Her* name.

The second jar. Oh, Lord! Clay's name.

"What's going on?"

"It appears that news travels around West Manhattan Saints as quickly as it did at my former hospital." His voice came from behind her. "They're betting on who's going to come out ahead during our exhibition match."

Her head whipped around to look at him. "Our exhibition? But that hasn't even been announced yet."

"Oh, it's been announced, all right. And it looks like there's no getting out of it at this point. I have a feeling Peter Lloyd isn't taking any chances. If this is as big a draw as he claims it will be, it'll be something for him to crow about."

All Tessa heard was the part about there being "no getting out of it at this point." Had Clay been trying to think of a way to not go through with the demonstration? She thought he'd resigned himself to it, just as she had. Evidently that wasn't the case.

"He can't do that. Besides, what's the point?"

"It seems he can and he did. All the money is still going to charity. It's just an internal bet with no actual payout. I've even heard talk of the hospital matching the donations of the winner's jar, although that would have to be approved by the hospital trustees."

How had he heard all of this when she had known nothing? "Maybe it was Marcos."

"Possibly, but I would lay odds on Lloyd. And so far it looks like you're ahead by a long shot. It seems you've engendered some loyalty, Dr. Camara."

She had? That was news to her. She was normally so busy she barely had time to throw a hello here or there. Which explained why she'd missed noticing those jars this morning.

Her sadness over Mr. Phillips was still hovering in the background, but even she could see the humor in this situation. "Well, you know... I think I've won every match we've ever fought."

"Because we weren't actually *supposed* to be fighting."

"Mmm-hmm."

"You don't sound convinced."

She smiled. "Because I'm not." Gesturing at the jars, she shrugged. "If this earns more money toward a good cause, then we'll just have to make sure we really do put on that good show we talked about."

"Are you saying you're going to take me down?"

Reaching into her side pocket, she took out a few bills and peeled off a ten. Walking over to the jars, she stuffed it inside the one with her name on it. She turned back to look at him. "Oh, yeah, mister. You are going down."

Dodge, dodge, dodge...retreat.

When was she going to miss a beat so that he could gain some ground?

Time and time again Tessa had pushed him to the very edge of the circle with no more than a twist of her body. She wasn't aiming to hit him, since that wasn't the goal of this match. But she was making him move his feet. And they sure as hell weren't moving forward.

They were supposed to be putting on a show, but not one that had him stepping backward for the whole fifteen minutes of their exhibition.

Cut yourself some slack.

This was only their first training match. He couldn't be expected to whip himself back into top form all at once.

Except his top form had never been any match for Tessa's skill. And she now had those damn jars as incentive to make this a show everyone would remember.

Well, two could play at that game.

Concentrate.

He sidestepped, mentally keeping the circle of people around them in his mind. He didn't want to go back so quickly that he careened into them—the idea was to stay inside the ring. If something happened the circle would open, but whoever broke it would automatically give up his place. In other words, he would lose.

Okay. He did a quick flip, a few muscles protesting at how much of a slacker he'd become over the past several years. His brain still remembered the moves, but his body was giving him hell over the contortions he was putting it through.

Tessa actually stepped out of the way.

One for me!

Until her foot found the back of his knee.

Dammit!

Down he went. Right onto his back.

He glared up at her, only to find her eyes alight with wicked laughter. She'd done that on purpose.

Just because she could.

And he found he couldn't stay mad at her. Not with her face all bright and gleeful and happy.

Happy.

He hadn't seen her like that in…over four years.

"Tessita." Marcos entered the circle. Unlike Tessa, the man did not look happy. "This is not what we are looking for. It is okay for one of you to defeat the other, but you need to give him more than two minutes. Otherwise those watching will not see the true beauty of our *capoeira*."

Ha! True. Two minutes did not constitute a match. Although his body could swear it had been closer to an hour. Marcos said it was okay for one of them to take the other down, but the director and Clay both knew who would be left standing and who would be on the floor when all was said and done. And that person was still grinning at him in that old familiar way—despite Marcos's chiding words.

Except this time it brought back a not-so-happy memory from days past, when she'd said the words that had ended their relationship. He'd lain flat on his figurative back then, too, while Tessa had stood over him, scowling. He'd do well to keep that in mind.

Clay levered himself to his feet. Lord, he was going to be sore tomorrow.

He waited for Marcos to leave the ring and for the rhythm instruments to again pick up that hypnotic beat. All the other participants had run their matches just as they'd been programmed, entering and exiting the ring like seasoned pros.

And he and Tessa—the last match on the exhibition agenda—were gumming up the works.

"Ready?" he asked.

"Absolutely." She yanked down the hem of her close-fitting tank top, her skin gleaming.

This time Clay executed a series of moves that actually had Tessa swerving and doing some tricky maneuvers of her own to avoid him getting too close.

This was more like it. For three minutes they continued like that, the match feeling much more even all of a sudden.

She arched into a backbend and flipped out of it like an expert.

Of course it felt even. Because she was letting him gain the upper hand. Just as Marcos had suggested.

Time and time again she kicked and bowed and spun. Back. Away from him.

"Dammit, Tessa, you're not even trying."

She swept by him with another grin. "Because someone told me to keep it going."

Perfect. She didn't have to admit to it.

He pushed harder. Entering her space and then

exiting it, his leg barely missing her head as he swept past. But Tessa was good at what she did, able to calculate down to the last centimeter how much room she needed to give him in order not to get hit. Because, as Marcos had said, the goal wasn't to make contact but to show off techniques and the unique dance style, the give and take that went on in the ring. Clay had never seen anything like it in his life. And the real *capoeira* experts were as ripped and fit as athletes in any other sport. The timing was what made it what it was. Because in some ways it was harder to go at each other knowing you weren't supposed to strike them, but to sweep past, and over, and under, with barely any room to spare. That took skill and an ability to read your opponent. Something Tessa seemed built to do.

And she *could* read him.

He only hoped that some of his secrets stayed hidden, even from the great Tessa Camara.

Like how turned on he got by watching her arms and legs move with the grace and strength of a ballerina.

At least when he wasn't the one fighting her.

And even now it was only his concentration that kept him from thinking too hard about her body and how absolutely flexible it was. In more ways than just training in *capoeira*.

Something hit the small of his back, and he lurched forward. Damn. He hadn't even seen that coming. And just like that he was once again on the defensive. Because Tessa had evidently decided enough time had gone by that she could really start fighting. And no way could he look down at his watch to see if the requisite fifteen minutes had passed. It probably had, though, because she would be keeping that internal clock ticking, despite gliding around the ring in time with the beat of the instruments.

His left knee gave way so fast that he thought he'd stepped the wrong way. He hadn't. Tessa had just stepped the right way. Down he went. For the second time that day.

Tessa once again stood over him, her exercise tank molding to her chest with each breath she took. "Sorry, Clay. You weren't concentrating."

No kidding.

Marcos clapped his hands. "This is enough

for tonight," he said, his Brazilian accent a little thicker than it had been at the start of the evening. "Much better, Tessa."

Oh, yeah? And what about him?

As if reading his thoughts, the other man said. "You will improve next time."

Clay, from his spot on the mat, couldn't help but chuckle. This was the same old Marcos. Never pampering his students but giving it to them straight, without being ugly. But his attempt at encouragement said it all. He would improve. He needed to improve. And the director would accept nothing less.

Hell, he'd missed this whole scene. More than he wanted to admit.

Tessa reached down to help him up. He started to ignore her hand but something made him grip her palm, making sure to give a quick jerk as he stood so that she was momentarily thrown against him. He stepped back. "Sorry, Tessa. That's what happens when I forget to concentrate."

Her face flashed with color immediately because he'd used those same words in more than just a *capoeira* session. He'd used them once when he'd been so carried away with how she'd made him feel that he'd lost control, coming in a rush before she'd climaxed.

He'd made it up to her minutes later, though, until her eyes had squeezed shut with her own orgasm.

And Clay had said those very words to explain what had happened.

She'd liked it. Liked that she could make him forget everything but what was happening.

Releasing her hand, he gave her a knowing smile. "Shall we call it even?"

Before she could say anything, Marcos was telling the group that he'd made plans for them all to go out to a bar a couple of blocks away to celebrate their first official practice session for the exhibition.

Clay could feign being tired and needing to go home and rest before work the next day, or say that Molly was waiting for him, but she was with his parents. Besides, he wanted to go. He'd missed the camaraderie of this group and how they always seemed to start their sessions as friends and leave the same way, no matter what went on in the ring. Maybe because they left any hard feelings inside that circle. Or maybe because most of them were Brazilian, lapsing into their own language at times. And they always made him feel like an insider—as part of them. Clay had learned bits and pieces of Portuguese during his time with Tessa, especially since her folks spoke it at home—although they'd always made an effort to speak English whenever he'd been around.

In the excited rush of voices that followed Marcos's announcement he glanced at Tessa and saw a shadow of indecision in her eyes. "Come on, Tess. You owe me a drink or two for the way you manhandled me."

Her brows went up. "Manhandled? I went easy on you."

Had she? A shadow passed through his head. Maybe she had tonight, but four years ago? Not a chance. And that should be what he concentrated on, not the memory of those times they'd shared in the ring…and in bed.

If only he could convince his body to cooperate.

He shook his head to rid it of that thought.

Today was a new day. And they could very well go out and enjoy a drink together, dammit, without him turning it into a huge friggin' deal.

The group headed to the locker rooms to change back into street clothes. Since Tessa was the only woman in the room, she went to Marcos's office.

Something about how close she and the studio owner seemed to be struck him for the first time.

He looked at Marcos with new eyes. Were they seeing each other outside these sessions? The man wasn't married, and he certainly seemed to have a soft spot for Tessa, having used the diminutive form of her name quite a bit today. He couldn't remember if Marcos had done that in the past.

But he was in his late forties.

And that meant what, exactly? Tessa was thirty. Not exactly a May to December romance.

A shard of what could have been jealousy went through him, except it wasn't. It couldn't be. He and Tessa had been over for a long time. He'd married another woman and had fathered a child, for heaven's sake. He saw how that had turned out. Failure on a spectacular level. So whatever was going on between Tessa and her trainer was none of his business.

She kissed you.

The inner voice rumbled in his head, reminding him that either he was wrong about his speculation or their relationship was open enough that neither of them cared what the other did.

He couldn't see Marcos being that nonchalant about it, though. He was a pretty intense man. And no way would Clay have ever allowed any man to touch Tessa without risking a permanently rearranged face when they'd been dating.

Again, those days were over.

He changed quickly and ran his fingers through his hair to put it back in some semblance of order.

Why? It was just Tessa and the old gang. They'd all just been through the same workout.

A few minutes later he was standing beside her as they made their way down the sidewalk. It had been decided it was faster to walk than to try to all pile into cars and meet there. Besides, The Pied Piper was only a couple of blocks away. And the way this group partied, it was probably better that no one would be driving himself home. They'd flag down taxis and return for their vehicles in the morning.

Clay intended to keep his wits about him, though, whatever the others decided to do. A night of drinking could cause problems and not just with his job.

"So is Molly going to come to the exhibition?" Tessa's question came out of nowhere.

"Probably. She seemed to like the studio a lot. My folks will be taking care of her during the festival, since I'll be a little occupied."

She immediately tensed, head coming up, eyes facing straight ahead. "That's nice. It's wonderful that they can watch her when her mother can't."

Yeah, which was most of the time, since Lizza was normally busy flitting here or there and focusing on her career. The funny thing about that was that Tessa was doing exactly the same thing. Working hard and putting all of her efforts into her job. But it didn't bother him that she did it.

Why?

Because if Molly had been her daughter, he had

no doubt that she would somehow make time for her, just as he did. Sure, his parents cared for her while he was working, but he spent every second he could with her. Tonight was the exception to the rule. He rarely went out to do anything fun anymore because he had responsibilities and he took them seriously.

So did Tessa.

And so did Lizza, in her own way. Except Molly's mother seemed to check her responsibilities at the door when it came to her own daughter.

His teeth grated against each other.

He glanced at Tessa, and she seemed to have relaxed again, so maybe it was his imagination that she'd suddenly gone all stiff and nonresponsive.

They arrived at the bar to find the *capoeira* group assembled out front. Marcos waited for the last two stragglers to arrive. "Everyone good with doing his own thing and leaving whenever you want? If you want to share cabs, make those arrangements now before it gets crazy. You can pair up again on the way out."

One of the players grinned. "My wife is meeting me here, so count me out. I'm not sharing that cab with anyone but her."

A couple of laughs went through the group at the bald innuendo.

Clay glanced at Tessa. "Are you okay with sharing one?"

"Of course." She stopped. "Unless you're staying until the place shuts down."

"I wasn't planning to. How about if we leave whenever you're ready?"

She gave him a pointed look. "If you want to prowl around, though, and find someone else to leave with, just let me know. You can text me."

"The only person I'm leaving with is you." He realized how that might have sounded when her face turned pink. But everyone was already moving into the bar and the sounds from inside were leaking out through the open door.

"I guess that's our cue. Shall we?"

He waited for her to enter, already ruing the thought of sharing a cab with her. Because it made him think of sharing other things. In a much more private and fulfilling venue. That single night of summer madness. The one he couldn't get out of his head.

A single night, he could probably handle. But any more than that truly would be madness.

CHAPTER NINE

SHE PROBABLY SHOULDN'T be dancing with him.

Especially not this kind of dancing. Cheek to cheek, her right hand cradled in his, the fingers of her left hand at the back of his neck. Except the entire evening had been leading up to this. She'd danced with Marcos for a whole dance before Clay had cut in with a smooth remark about needing to discuss *capoeira* strategy for the exhibition.

Only Clay hadn't talked strategy. He'd simply spun her into his arms as a slow dance came on, his warm fingers burning through the thin knit top she'd changed into. It wasn't nightclub wear, since she hadn't known they'd be going out tonight. But, then again, The Pied Piper wasn't a dressy kind of club. It was where professionals went after work to wind down from the day. And to possibly score a little company for the night.

Tessa wasn't interested in scoring anything. So she'd been more than happy to stick to dancing with people she knew. Even if that meant finding herself in Clay's arms all over again. They'd come to this club from time to time when they'd had a few hours free during med school, which hadn't been often. But when they had, they'd inevitably wound up in a bed somewhere. Once they hadn't even made it that far, driving Clay's little sports car to a secluded spot across the Jersey border and squeezing both of their bodies into the passenger seat.

Sex between them had always been hot.

Which was why she wondered what she'd been thinking to allow herself to fall right back into his embrace.

She wasn't. Thinking, that was.

It was the excitement of fighting him in the circle once again. The memories of how invigorating those matches could become later, in the privacy of the night.

Which made her next thought stop her in her tracks. What would it matter if they engaged in a little hanky-panky on the side? They were no longer involved—Clay had a young daughter he needed to concentrate on.

But she had needs. And she imagined he did, too—although Clay probably had those needs met on a regular basis. She wasn't made like that. But maybe she could bend her own rules in this case, since she and Clay weren't exactly strangers.

Her fingers tightened a bit on his neck. Clay's response was to grip her waist with a firmer hand. Or maybe that was her imagination wanting to make it so.

And, Lord, if he didn't smell good. Too good. Especially this close. The match and exertion should have washed away any trace of aftershave, so that couldn't be the source of the woodsy, yummy scent that made her breathe a little bit deeper.

It was just Clay. She recognized it—remembered going to sleep to it and waking up with it beneath her skin. And, just like in the past, it drew her to him.

Her nose brushed his shoulder before she realized how close she'd gotten to him. With almost no hesitation—except maybe in her brain—her head turned sideways and she pressed her cheek against him, allowing her eyes to close. To "feel." Something she hadn't done in a very long time.

Her days of med school and internship had turned her into an analytical machine, with cause and effect always at the forefront of her mind… her feelings tucked in a distant part of her brain, where they rarely surfaced. Except in instances like with Mr. Phillips, when they'd reemerged without warning and threatened her objectivity.

Maybe she shouldn't even be a doctor.

Yes, she should. Her mom had been so excited for her when she'd been accepted into med school.

And if it had come with a price—her relationship to Clay—it was still worth it.

If she could help people like Mr. Phillips, then she would continue to make those sacrifices.

The hand at her waist slid backward until it rested on the small of her back. She might have thought he was trying to put some distance between them but, if anything, he was tucking her closer, his chin coming down to rest on top of her head.

Her breath caught at the familiarity that was slowly wrapping her in cords of silk.

Especially with the little hum of vibration that went through his chest, a sound she couldn't hear but that she could feel. And she felt it all the way down to her toes.

What was one night? Was Clay even thinking the same thing? Wondering if they could set the love machine for a quick tumble cycle that would heat up quickly, shaking out the wrinkles from their daily lives? Afterward they could fold everything up and put it back into a drawer. Out of sight. Out of mind.

Should she say something? Proposition him?

And just where would this sexathon take place? She could drag him back to her unit at the brownstone, where Caren, Holly or Sam might overhear something. Her nose crinkled. No, if they got together, she didn't want to hold back anything, except her emotions.

They could go to his place—where he'd murmured he wanted to take her when they kissed in

Central Park. His apartment was empty—at least according to Clay, who'd said that Molly would be at his parents' house for the night.

She tilted her head, dislodging his chin. He glanced down, a frown marring his brow.

"Do you think Marcos would mind if we left early?" she asked.

"Marcos?" His eyebrows pulled closer together as he studied her for a second or two. "Feeling okay?"

"Not really." That wasn't what she'd meant to say. She hurried to correct herself. "I'm feeling a little…"

Her courage gave out, and she let her voice trail away.

"A little what? You've only had a glass of wine, not very much, even for a featherweight like you." This time a slight smile edged one side of his mouth, although his frown was still there.

"No, it's not the wine." Wow, she was glad she wasn't a man, because she was terrible at this pickup stuff. They could have it. "I was just wondering if you might want to…"

She swallowed and forced the rest of the words out. "Leave. Go somewhere else."

His face went totally still, and she held her breath, praying that if he was going to refuse he would at least let her down easily.

"You're not going to believe this, but I was thinking the very same thing."

"Oh, God." She sagged against him. "It's stupid, isn't it? We shouldn't. We both know it."

"Yes. My head knows it." He hauled her closer, where she could feel the inner workings of a certain body part. "But other areas disagree. Vehemently, I might add."

"Ditto on both counts."

His hand slid beneath her hair and held her while his mouth came down and claimed hers.

Lord, she hoped no one in their party could see them now. But if Clay wasn't worried about it, why should she be?

She kissed him back, stretching up as high as she could in order to reach him better. It wasn't enough. What they both needed was a surface that put them on a level playing field.

Like a bed.

Something on Clay's body vibrated again. Only this time it didn't come from his chest but his waistline.

She broke free. "Clay…"

"I know. Give me a sec." He unclipped his cell phone with one hand while keeping her tight against him with the other. He put the object to his ear. "Matthews here."

The frown was back. Not of confusion this time but of concern. "Where are you?"

She thought at first it was his parents saying something had happened to Molly, except his face was up looking over the heads of the people on the dance floor. When she turned to follow his lead she saw a hand waving.

"Got it," he said. "We'll be right there. Call 911 as soon as you hang up."

He let go of her and shoved his phone back in its holder. He leaned down so she could hear him above the music. "Something's wrong with Marcos. Let's go."

Her heart in her throat, she kept hold of Clay's hand as he led the way toward the place where she'd seen the hand waving. As soon as they arrived, she dropped to her knees.

Marcos was having a seizure, eyes rolled back, muscles twitching in useless contractions. The connections in his brain were going haywire.

Why?

She went back into analytical mode as she tilted the *capoeira* master's head to the side in case he vomited, while Clay belted out question after question about whether or not anyone knew Marcos's medical history. More *capoeira* folks had evidently noticed that something was going on, because they slowly gathered around them, including the man who'd mentioned sharing a cab with his wife. He was the one who finally spoke. "He has epilepsy."

What?

Tessa looked down at the man she'd known most of her life. She glanced at his wrist, but there was no medical alert bracelet, something he should have been wearing. But Marcos was a proud man. And Brazilians didn't like to display weakness. She remembered one of her father's friends who'd severed his index finger at the second joint. He'd insisted the doctor reattach it, even though the digit would never bend again but would stick straight out. He'd just wanted to "be whole."

Clay asked their group to form a ring around Marcos just like during practice to keep everyone back and then knelt beside her.

She glanced at her watch, timing the length of the seizure. Two minutes from the time Clay's phone had rung. If it lasted longer than five minutes, they were in trouble. Right now, though, they were helpless to do anything except wait it out and hope that an ambulance arrived soon.

"What does he take?" Her eyes went to the man who'd voiced that Marcos had epilepsy.

He shrugged. "I don't know. I just saw something on the calendar on his desk about a doctor's appointment. I asked, and he told me. I had no idea until a couple of years ago."

Marcos went still suddenly, all his muscles going lax. Glancing at her watch again, she murmured, "Just over three minutes from the time you got the call."

Despite the medical emergency, the music was

still playing and there was activity on the dance floor. Not everyone knew something had happened on this side of the room, which was probably a good thing, since she could just barely hear the sound of an ambulance in the distance.

A man in a tie broke through the ring and stood over them, introducing himself as The Pied Piper's owner. "What happened?"

Clay spoke up. "We're doctors and our friend had a seizure. There's an ambulance en route. If you can clear a path to the door and let the EMTs get through, we'd appreciate it."

All it took was a motion from the owner to get three beefy men to come over. He explained and they immediately opened up a swath of space. Within another minute a duo came through, wheeling a stretcher.

Marcos was just starting to regain consciousness, trying to weakly wave away their attempts to help.

Tessa leaned close to him and whispered in his ear that he needed to go with the EMTs and get checked out at the hospital. "Did you take your meds?"

He blinked at her as if he might deny taking anything, then nodded. "Yes."

The medical services pair quickly took her friend's vitals and checked his pupils, asking a few standard questions about whether he'd hit his head and how much he'd had to drink. Marcos was still too confused to really answer much, so they put a collar around his neck just in case and bundled him back through the crowd on the gurney, with Tessa following close behind. Clay turned to talk to the other guys from the studio, probably reassuring them that he'd let them know what was going on as soon as he knew something. He caught up with her just as they reached the ambulance. The EMTs recognized her from the hospital, so they didn't question her when she said they'd meet them at the hospital.

Then the ambulance was off and Clay was flagging down a taxi.

There was silence on the way to the hospital. Her stomach churned in her gut as her thoughts raced. Marcos had epilepsy? He was a *grande mestre* in *capoeira*, a level that took many years and a whole lot of training to reach. She couldn't believe someone hadn't discovered this sooner, although most epileptics whose seizure activity was well controlled could live normal lives and do most of the things that other people did. Except drive. And even that depended on the type of seizure activity.

But Tessa had never seen any evidence of even a petit mal seizure.

A taxi pulled up to the curb and they both got in.

Clay wrapped an arm around her waist and slid her next to him. "Sorry, honey. He's confused right now. Maybe he forgot to take his meds this morning. And if he had anything to drink…"

"I know." She laid her head on his shoulder. "Anything could have triggered it. We'll have to wait and see what he says when he's a little more with it."

"I know he's special to you."

She closed her eyes. "Yes. Very."

Warm fingers cupped her chin and lifted her head. "How 'very' is very?"

What did he mean? "I've known Marcos my whole life. I've been at that studio since I was a kid. Marcos took over as owner when I was a teenager."

"Is there something more to it than that?"

"More…?" She sat straight up, eyes widening. "What the hell, Clay? Do you think I would have asked you to leave the club with me if there was anything going on between me and Marcos?"

His fingers tightened to prevent her from jerking away. Instead, she glared up at him, anger pulsing at her temples. "The way he talks to you…"

"We're friends. He's friends with my parents." She shook her head. "Just like your parents and mine are friends."

"Exactly."

She sighed, her indignation beginning to unravel at the seams. "He's almost twenty years older than me."

"Since when has that mattered?"

She could see his point. But her and Marcos?

It was true that she and Clay had originally met through their parents—at a Christmas party his folks had thrown years earlier. The second they'd seen each other it had all been over. And when they'd danced…

She and Marcos had never shared that same

spark. Not when they first met…and not after all these years of working together. She saw him as a mentor. Someone to learn from.

"We're friends." She placed a little more emphasis on the words this time around.

They pulled up to the hospital, and she was the first to leap out of the cab, hurrying up the walkway while he had to stop and pay the driver for the short ride. Even so, he caught up with her before she reached the double doors of the emergency room. "Wait."

She slowed her pace. "You can go ahead and go home. He's my friend. I'm going to check on him."

"He's my friend, too." Once they were through the doors he stopped in front of her. "It was an honest question. If we were going to go back to my place, I wanted to know the score. I don't encroach on anyone's territory."

"I can't believe you just said that. I'm no one's territory."

He laughed. "No. You're not. You were always your own woman. Someone who knew exactly what she wanted out of life."

A flash of hurt went through her heart. At one time that "want" had included Clay.

"No more than anyone else."

There wasn't any time to say more because one of the ER doctors met them in the hallway, nodding a greeting at them. She quickly explained why they were there. "Marcos Figuereiro. The man who came in with epilepsy."

"Dr. Simon is back there with him right now. Exam room three, I think."

They made their way to the cubicle and Tessa called through the closed curtain. "Drs. Camara and Matthews are here to see Marcos."

"Come in. We're just getting some background on him." Randy Simon's words came through loud and clear. A large man with a booming tone and optimistic manner, he was good with patients and family alike.

Clay drew back the curtain and motioned her in first, then followed her. Dr. Simon draped his stethoscope around his neck and glanced up at them.

"He has epilepsy?"

Marcos growled, "I am right here."

"So you are." Randy's brows went up an inch, but he smiled down at the man and went back and forth with him about his diagnosis and medical history. It was like pulling teeth, though, to get anything out of the man.

But they did eventually. Dr. Simon decided to hold him overnight and check the blood levels of his meds. Marcos grumbled about it all, but Tessa got the feeling the episode had scared him as much as it had those around him. Which meant it wasn't something that happened every day. So, yes, it was better to make sure nothing had changed or that there wasn't something else insidious going on inside her friend's body.

"You two might as well go home." Marcos crossed his strong arms over his chest. "I'll probably get the worst night's sleep known to man, but I would rather do it in private than have someone hover over me for the next eight hours."

"Are you sure?"

"I will call if I need something."

Tessa managed a smile. "Hope you don't mind if I don't believe you."

She reached into her purse—realizing for the

first time that Clay must have retrieved it from their table at The Pied Piper, as she'd forgotten all about it until they were in the cab. But there it had been. She found a business card and wrote her cell phone number on the back of it, handing it to Dr. Simon. "Will you have someone call me if something changes?"

He glanced from her to Clay, probably wondering what they were doing out and about together. Those damned jars. She vaguely remembered seeing a pair of them in the ER, as well.

Perfect.

"I'll give you a call," he assured her.

Clay shook the other doctor's hand while she leaned down to kiss Marcos's cheek.

"You get some rest," she said. "We have a lot more practicing to do over the next couple of weeks, and we need you strong and rested."

He grumbled about them needing a lot more than a couple weeks, but since that was all they had…

They left, and Tessa wasn't sure what to do. Did she hang around in the waiting room to see if there was any news? Or did she go home?

Now that the scare was over, she was wide-awake. There was no way she'd get any sleep tonight.

A vision of herself wrapped in Clay's strong arms shimmied through her head, bringing with it the knowledge that she'd never had insomnia when they'd spent the nights together. Instead, she'd slept like a baby.

Clay, as if reading her thoughts, said, "You can't do anything by waiting around, Tess. Randy said he'd call if something changed." He glanced at his watch. "Besides, it's almost eleven."

Too late to do anything besides sleep? Yes, he was probably hinting that his better sense had put in an appearance after all and that he wanted to go home. Alone.

The least she could do was be graceful about it if that was the case, although now that Marcos's doctor had her cell phone number she would love nothing more than to go to sleep with Clay next to her. But she wouldn't.

"Well, I guess I'll see you tomorrow, then?"

They stepped through the emergency room

doors into the balmy night air. "That depends on how long you plan on staying over."

"Staying over?" Said as if her heart had not just leaped in her chest at the idea that he might not be saying good-night quite yet after all.

His eyes narrowed. "Nothing's changed, Tessa. And if I know you, you won't get any sleep." He wrapped his hand around her nape. "I still want you to come home with me. Will you?"

He was asking. Not demanding. Not assuming, as he might have when they'd been together before.

Relief washed through her. "Yes. If you're sure."

"Honey, I'd like nothing better than to be pinned down by you in circumstances other than standing in a roomful of men watching our every move."

Capoeira.

She grinned, her eyes holding his as her fears over Marcos began to fade. "You just don't like to lose in front of a bunch of people."

"I don't like to lose at all. But what I have in

mind has two winners and zero losers. And no one around to see the outcome except for us."

He drew her a little closer and then bent down to give her a light kiss.

Unfortunately, he didn't move to deepen the contact, and considering they were standing outside the hospital, that was a good thing. For both of them.

He didn't release his hold on her, however. So his next words were whispered inches away from her lips, giving them an intimacy she was dying to explore.

"My place. My bed." The promise from a week ago flowed over her skin, making her shiver.

"Your car?" She didn't have a vehicle at the moment, preferring to zip around the huge city on public transport or her own two feet.

"I think we can make it to the apartment."

Only after he'd said it did she realize he'd taken her question about how they were going to get to his place and expanded it to include whether or not they would even make it that far. Or whether they'd have to park his car and consummate things inside. As they'd done before.

An ambulance pulled into the circular drive in a blare of sirens and Clay finally lifted his head and backed up a pace. But he didn't leave her totally without contact. Reaching down, he grabbed her hand, tugging her to his side. "Ready?"

She made a sound of affirmation that found her being towed behind him, his long steps requiring two of hers for every one of his. She didn't care. All she knew was that she was going to feel him around her in a way that she hadn't in four long years.

And she couldn't wait.

Maybe they wouldn't make it back to his apartment after all.

She managed to climb into his car with shaky legs and settle into place. She even managed to keep her hands to herself, although she couldn't say the same of Clay. Because once they got out of the parking lot and onto the street, they were immediately caught up in a snarl of traffic that slowed to a crawl.

"Damn," he muttered.

Double damn, she echoed in her head. Balling her hands together in her lap, she tried not to squirm on the leather upholstery beneath her thighs. Or dwell on the warm ache between those very same thighs.

Clay let go of the gearshift and dropped his palm onto her left leg, just above her knee. "This wasn't quite what I had in mind, but…"

Her breath caught in her throat when his thumb brushed over the loose, gauzy fabric of her long skirt. The ache grew a little stronger.

The car in front of them crept forward a couple of inches, and Clay followed it, the slow pace evidently not requiring him to shift, since his hand stayed right where it was. In fact, his fingers ran in little waves of motion along her inner thigh in a way that caused the hem of her skirt to rise almost to her knee, where he caught it with his index finger and lifted it higher.

"Clay?" His name came out a bit strangled.

"Shh…" This time when his fingertips came back in contact with her it was against bare skin. "Who knows how long this ride is going to last? Just keeping you interested."

Interested? She didn't need him to do anything to hold her enthralled. And the only ride she wanted right now was one where she was straddling his hips and moaning.

His windows were darkly tinted, and between the streetlights and headlights she doubted anyone could see inside the vehicle. Still, when his hand changed legs and bunched the fabric up until it was halfway between her knees and her hips, her stomach tightened in anticipation, along with everything else.

He dragged his palm with painful slowness up her skin, raising goose bumps in its wake, his eyes never leaving the road. And yet, even without glancing at her once, he seemed to know the havoc he was wreaking on her mind…and her body.

Traffic moved forward another couple of feet, and suddenly Tessa wasn't in such a hurry to arrive at their destination.

He continued to tease with light strokes up… down…across, never quite reaching his destination. Eventually, she couldn't take it any longer and her eyelids slammed shut, unable to concentrate on anything other than what Clay was doing, how he made her feel.

And it was incredible. She trusted him not to go so far that he would get them both arrested, even as she turned her body over to him, allowing him to do things she never would have let anyone else do.

Because she did trust him.

Wanted him.

Despite their past.

And when he got them home she was going to show him exactly how much.

His fingers slid between her thighs and urged them a few inches apart with a gentle pressure that she immediately responded to, although she did have enough common sense to reach down and flip the fabric of her skirt down over his hand and her knees.

"No fair, Tessa." He ventured higher, wringing an unwilling moan from her throat, her head lolling back against the seat. "I'm beginning to think I should have chosen the car option."

She felt the vehicle move forward again. Each time it did, Clay seemed to grow a little bolder.

When he withdrew his hand completely, though, her eyes jerked open in disappointment.

"Truck," he murmured, as a big vehicle rumbled forward and moved twenty yards ahead of them.

Thinking she'd give him a taste of his own medicine, she twisted on her seat and moved her hand to the gearshift, sliding her fingers over the top of it and then down its stem, watching him. He wasn't looking but she knew he was aware of exactly what she was doing—of the game she was playing.

"Dangerous."

"No more dangerous than what you were doing," she whispered.

"I'm driving."

Yeah, driving me insane. She didn't say it out loud, though, because it sounded stupid, even to her own ears. But it was true. And Clay knew it was. He always did somehow, even when she'd tried to hide how devastating his touch was to her. And when he'd shown up at her dorm room she'd kept the door between them, knowing that if he touched her it was all over.

It always would be for her.

That fact should make her wary, should make

her back away from him emotionally, even now. That's what she was trying to do, actually. Accept that they'd always been more than compatible physically, even if they weren't good as life partners.

She needed to be self-sufficient. He'd tended to smother…trying to take care of her, even when she'd longed to do things herself.

Traffic opened up suddenly, and Clay spent the next few minutes threading his vehicle through the congestion, making several turns before finally veering into the parking garage of what looked like an exclusive apartment building.

Of course it would be.

Even as the thought ran through her mind, she banished it. The brownstone she lived in wasn't exactly a pauper's abode, thanks to Holly's family. Besides, tonight wasn't about houses or money or anything else. It was about her needs and Clay's needs and how they could come together to find a mutually satisfying solution.

The second he pulled his car into a space and shut off the engine he threaded his fingers through her hair and turned her face up for his kiss. And as soon as his lips met hers she knew there was no turning back. She and Clay were destined to reignite the fires of the past. She just hoped that when it was all over she'd have the strength and courage to put them out again.

CHAPTER TEN

TOUCHING HER MADE something inside him come alive.

And at the moment he wasn't touching anything except her hand as they rode up in the elevator. But she was gripping back as if her very life depended on maintaining that contact.

If someone had told him four years ago that he'd find himself riding to his apartment with this woman, he'd have said they were crazy.

But maybe he was the crazy one. Setting himself up for another big knock to the gut.

Nope. No gut involved. Just that single night of summer madness he'd been craving for what seemed like ages. Nothing below skin level would be involved. Because anything she touched would be on the surface. No emotions. No longing. Just skin-to-skin contact that he could wash off with a single quick spray of his showerhead. Just like soap or shampoo. Once applied, he would simply rinse it all off again.

But didn't most of the instructions on those packages say "Lather, rinse...*repeat*"?

Maybe one night should become two.

He tugged her closer, until their arms were touching. As long as he was smart about this, he could have sex with her as many times as he wanted and not be affected. After all, when Lizza had finally filed for divorce, it hadn't hurt that much. In fact, he'd been relieved in some ways, except for the fact that Molly had been left without a mom for the most part.

He'd had superficial sex since then. Not very often, because he did have a daughter to think of. But the times he had, he'd been able to roll from beneath the woman's sheets and get on with his life without a backward glance.

Except he hadn't brought them to his place. He and Lizza had never even lived in this apartment. His home had become sacrosanct...a place reserved for him and Molly only.

So what was different now? He was about to

violate his own unspoken rule: no liaisons of the sexual kind happened in the apartment. Ever.

Madness.

To keep from trying to rationalize things beyond that one word, he let go of her hand and draped his arm around her shoulders, allowing his fingertips to glide across the bare skin of her arm. On the second pass he moved the contact forward just a couple of inches, so that he was still on her arm, but the backs of his knuckles grazed the outside of her breast as he made his way back down. A shiver went through her.

The elevator stopped on his floor before he could do anything more.

And there was still a whole lot he wanted to do.

He spun her out of the elevator and against the door of his apartment, settling his mouth on hers in a way that he hoped left no question about what they were going to do. It wasn't as if he thought she was going to angle for a cup of coffee and then flee for her life. But why take any chances?

When her palms landed on his butt, fingers splayed apart and urging him closer, he combusted, a flame shooting from his groin to the top of his head. She was evidently taking no chances, either.

He obliged her, pushing one knee between her legs and settling his stiff flesh against her thigh. Digging into his pocket for his key, he managed to get it into the lock beside her waist and twisted. The door gave way, and so did Tessa, tumbling to the hardwood floor and dragging him down with her. He was somehow able to keep from crushing her as he landed, her husky laugh washing over him in a flood he just couldn't resist. So he stayed there, pushing the door shut with the sole of his shoe as he sank deeper into her soft curves, his aching flesh wanting nothing more than to yank her skirt up and be done with it. To hell with all the formalities.

But if he hurried it would be over.

As in…no second chances.

So he tried to rein himself in, thinking he would stand up calmly and lead her to the bedroom. But Tessa's hands were on his ass again, only this time they'd somehow wormed their way beneath his waistband and briefs and were now on his bare skin. Her mouth found his at the same time, and he knew it was all over, because her kiss was warm and thorough, shot through with sensual promise.

He gave it one last shot. "My bedroom is just down the hallway."

Her fingers traveled lower, setting off another set of explosions within his skull. Then she pulled her hands free. But before he could protest she shoved him up and over, until he was the one on his back and she was straddling his hips.

"Damn, Tess, if you wanted to be in charge, all you had to do was ask."

She leaned over, elbows beside his shoulders, her breath washing over his lips. "I prefer to keep my opponent off guard."

Hell if she hadn't done that the whole time he'd known her. When she leaned over and gave his lower lip a quick bite, sucking it, his eyes closed as a wave of ecstasy swept over him.

"So I'm the opponent?" His voice came out rough, sounding very much as he felt—that what little control he had was rapidly crumbling.

She sat up and pulled her shirt over her head,

revealing a tiny black bra that barely covered the tops of her breasts. "If you fight me on this, absolutely."

"Honey, I have no intention of fighting anything." He decided to have some fun of his own, reaching up to take hold of the fabric barely holding in her curves and tugging it down to expose them completely. "I just thought you might want a soft bed to do this in."

Her fingers trailed along his jawline and one brow edged up. "I don't want a soft…anything."

To prove her point, she widened her legs and settled fully against him, shifting her hips along his length.

No softness there. Just a pulsing need that wouldn't quit.

Tessa balled her skirt up and allowed it to rest on the tops of her thighs, baring them, while she reached for the button of his slacks.

"Wait." He gritted out the word. "I told you I don't want this to be a quickie. I want to enjoy you."

"After getting me all worked up in the car as we drove here? No chance. And, believe me, I intend to enjoy it. Fully. Deeply." The button popped free, and his zip went down. "And I somehow think you'll manage to come along for the ride."

At the rate she was going it would be a very short trip. But if that's the way she wanted it, who was he to turn her down?

Then she had him in her hands. Squeezing. Stroking. Driving him out of his mind.

"Condom."

"Pill."

"In that case…" He took hold of her butt with both hands and lifted her slightly, waiting for her to hold herself in that position. Then he reached beneath her skirt and found her panties. Moist heat met his touch as he edged aside the silky fabric. "Let's see just how fully and deeply we can go."

He guided himself into position. She immediately pushed down hard until she was fully seated, a soft sound coming from her lips as she paused there. "Damn."

Damn? *Damn?*

"Too deep?" Afraid he was hurting her, he

started to reach for her, only to have her wave away his hands.

"No. Too good." She sat very still, her bared breasts rising and falling as she breathed in and out, mouth open, eyes closed.

Hadn't she just suggested that she was going to make him pay for what he'd done in the car?

Too late for you to try to draw things out now, darling.

And he was going to make sure she suffered as much as he was suffering. One hand went to her breast and the other beneath her skirt, both finding their targets within seconds.

Her eyes flashed open. "Wh-what are you doing?"

"Keeping my opponent off guard." With that he pressed up deeper with his hips and used his thumb to glide over that most sensitive part of her.

Tessa moaned. "No, I won't be able to—"

"Don't, then, baby. Let it go."

He kept up his assault, stoking with his hands and pumping with his hips, until she joined him, riding him, her hands on his shoulders.

A few seconds later her movements became jerky and erratic, fingertips digging into his skin.

Yes!

She cried out, and her flesh clenched down tight on him, sending a searing stream of pleasure through his system that he no longer tried to fight. Instead, he released his hold, his own orgasm breaking free with a violent series of spasms that made his vision go dark for several long seconds.

When he finally came back to himself Tessa was half lying across his chest, one arm curled around the top of his head.

They were a tangled mess of clothing and limbs.

And Clay wouldn't have had it any other way.

Or maybe he would. Because he wasn't done with her. Not yet.

So, keeping the contact between their bodies, he rolled her beneath him, his body already responding to the thoughts that were beginning to filter through his head. "Let's say we try that again. Only this time in my bed. And without our clothes."

She smiled up at him and the pure contentment on her face sent a twinge of warning through him that he ignored.

"What fun would that be?" she murmured.

"Oh, I bet we can figure something out. And I promise I can make it a whole lot of fun."

Tessa actually laughed. "Then lead the way. And if you think I'm not going to hold you to that promise, buster, you're very much mistaken."

They had a small going-away party for Caren, just the housemates. But it was hard to concentrate on sending her friend off when her mind was on what she'd done last night with Clay. They'd made love several times and it had taken her until tonight when she'd opened up her packet of birth control pills to realize there were three extra pills in her little round compact.

She'd missed taking them the past three nights. Three!

That had happened a couple of times over the past six months, but as she hadn't been sleeping with anyone she hadn't worried about it. Her night shifts always threw her schedule off, and it had been a crazy couple of weeks. Every other time she'd simply caught up with her dosage and gone on with life.

She swallowed as the implication hit her.

This wasn't "every other time."

Clay had offered to use a condom.

Why hadn't she let him?

She'd been too caught up in her own greedy need to get him inside her, and she had no idea if the condom he'd talked about had been in his wallet or in another room of the house. And she hadn't wanted him to get up.

Besides, she was on the Pill! Or she had been. And she hadn't planned on spending the *entire* night at his place. She'd figured she'd just take it when she got home.

Panic flashed through her system. What if his sperm had already made its way to an egg?

Would taking a Pill now undo it all? Maybe.

Which is what you need to do!

Or there *were* morning-after pills. That might be the best route.

But hadn't she been thinking about adoption or in vitro once her residency was completed?

The image of herself holding Clay's baby began growing in her head.

What if this was fate's way of telling her to go for it? That now was the time?

And what about Clay? Did he have no say in the matter? She didn't know. Her emotions were a huge jumbled knot in her stomach.

She needed to give herself a few hours or a day to think this through. It wasn't as if she had to decide in the next fifteen minutes.

Really?

God, she was setting herself up for a disaster. She was almost at the end of her residency—there was no way she could afford a pregnancy right now.

And especially not one with a man she'd ended things with four years ago.

What a mess.

Caren touched her arm. "Everything okay?"

"Yes. Of course it is." She searched her mind for a believable reason for being so distant. "I'm just thinking about the festival. There are only two more weeks to get ready for it."

"I know. You must be nervous. And it's weird

about those jars, but I'm sure it's just some dummy playing around." She winked.

Holly nodded, lowering her voice so that Sam, who was busy pouring their drinks, wouldn't hear. "You know how things get blown out of proportion."

"What things?" She had no idea what either of them were talking about.

The two women looked at each other. "The jars. The ones of you and Dr. Matthews," Holly whispered. "Someone added something to them."

"Added what?" Tessa had been far too distracted, her head racing with other, more pressing, worries.

Caren's brows went up. "You haven't seen them yet?"

She'd been too confused today to even look at them. Actually, she'd been avoiding looking at them like the plague. Because she somehow had to get up the nerve to keep on practicing with him or she'd have a lot of explaining to do to Peter Lloyd. And to Marcos. No way did she want to tell anyone what had happened between them last night.

Clay's mom had shown up at eight o'clock this morning with Molly in tow. Tessa had been in the shower, still in a blissful haze after waking up to Clay's lips on her neck. Only the Clay who'd poked his head into the bathroom had been a different man from the one who'd sunk into her two hours earlier. "My mom is here with Molly."

Her heart had shuddered to a stop. "*Meu Deus.* What do you want me to do?"

She'd expected him to tell her to hide under the bed until he could sneak her out of the house. Instead, he'd shaken his head. "Nothing. I told them we had an emergency at the hospital and were exhausted. That you slept over." He gave her a smile. "You were expecting to hide in a closet?"

Yes.

She brought herself back to the conversation at hand. Which she couldn't seem to remember for the life of her. Oh, yeah. The collection jars. "We found out that the hospital administrator set them up. Are they overflowing or something?"

Holly glanced again at Sam, who was now headed toward them, juggling four glasses. "Just look at them when you get to the hospital in the morning, okay? You'd think that you and Dr. Matthews were dating."

She sucked down a shocked breath, but before she could say anything else Sam was handing her a cranberry juice—she'd refused the wine, saying she wasn't feeling all that well. Poor Caren. This wasn't exactly the send-off she'd been looking to give her. And she would genuinely miss her.

"So when does Kimberlyn arrive again?"

"She's supposed to start moving in the day of the festival, so I figure it'll be a good way for her to see some of the hospital staff in a more laid-back setting." Caren looked around at the group. "Make her feel welcome, okay? She's been putting a lot of pressure on herself lately. If she doesn't get that fellowship…"

Tessa laid a hand on her arm. "Don't worry, we'll make sure she feels at home. We'll put up a sign and everything."

Holly smiled, dropping onto one of the plush striped sofas that flanked the fireplace and taking a sip of her wine.

"I can tell her where all the cool shops are, or go with her if she needs anything. You just make sure you don't catch any tropical diseases, or we'll have to come down and rescue you."

"I'll be careful. Don't get rid of my room or anything. I plan on taking up where I left off when I get back next year."

This time Sam spoke up, his eyes glinting. "I'll try to keep Holly from redecorating it while you're gone." Their male housemate might be quiet but his dry humor sometimes came out of nowhere, surprising them all.

They all laughed right on cue, and Sam emptied his glass of the last of his wine. "I can't stay but, seriously, take care, kiddo. And keep in touch."

"I will." She gave him a hug. "I need to go, too. Would you mind lugging those two bags to the bottom of the stairs while I call a cab?"

"Will do." Sam took his wineglass and set it on the counter by the sink. To Holly and Tessa he said, "See you sometime tonight."

With that, he picked up their friend's luggage as if it weighed nothing and headed out the door.

Tessa's eyes moistened. "I'm going to miss you. More than you know."

"I know. Me, too. But I'll be back before you know it. Give Kimber any help she needs, okay?"

Holly gave Caren a quick hug as well, turning away quickly, probably on the verge of blubbering, just as Tessa was. "I'll call the taxi service for you."

Moving forward, Tessa gave her friend a long hug, feeling sadder than she should under the circumstances. This was a fabulous opportunity for Caren, and she should be glad for her.

She was. She was just feeling weepy and out of sorts for some reason today.

"Email me as soon as you can. And call if you need anything."

"You can count on it, honey. Don't go and get married or anything before I get back."

That was one thing she could reassure Caren about. "I'm not planning on marrying anyone for a long, long time. Maybe even never. I have too much to prove to myself first."

If things hadn't gone south between her and Clay, she might already be married. But their relationship might have wound up on the rocks, like his other marriage. Part of Tessa wondered if she was even marriage material. She squirmed at the thought of a man wanting to protect her. Or pay her way.

She felt for any guy who ended up getting involved with her.

Caren glanced at her face and then smiled. "Be careful about saying never. And definitely look at those jars when you go to work tomorrow. And I hereby deny all knowledge."

Something about the way she'd said that…

"Knowledge of what? Caren, what did you do?"

Holly came back over. "Taxi is en route."

"Saved by the cab. Okay, I'll go stand with my luggage so Sam doesn't have to wait around. Love you guys."

"Love you, too," Tessa and Holly said.

Holly turned to her. "I need to run by the hospital and check on my schedule for next week."

"I'll straighten up." Tessa was actually glad to be by herself for a few minutes. She'd been running on nerves since she left Clay's this morning. Maybe she could take a bath in peace for once. It had been a long time, in fact, since she'd had a day off. It was sorely needed today of all days.

And it might give her a chance to figure out what to do, or at least work up the courage to do something that would make sure she wasn't pregnant.

She waved the girls off and slumped into one of the chairs, where she sat for several minutes, just staring at the empty fireplace in front of her.

Her eyes closed and her hand slid across her tummy. "Please, God, don't let me have to make that choice. Anything but that."

A gust of wind blew against one of the windows, making it rattle in its frame. Somehow she couldn't get it out of her mind that the Big Guy might just be looking down at her and laughing.

Clay was in the lobby when she arrived at work the next morning. And the man did not look happy.

Her stomach clenched, but she forced a smile. "Hi. You're here early." Tessa had purposely arrived a half hour before her shift. Obviously, if she'd been trying to avoid Clay, her plan had failed miserably.

And she still hadn't started taking her her birth

control pills, because she didn't know if it would do any good at this point. But what she *had* done was decide to make an appointment with the head of Maternal Fetal medicine here at the hospital and see what she had to say.

You would think as a doctor Tessa could formulate her own professional opinion. And she could, medically speaking. But it wouldn't be objective. And that's what she needed right now, someone to talk her off whatever ledge she was standing on.

Clay still wasn't smiling. "I need to warn you about something."

This time it wasn't her stomach muscles that reacted but her heart, the organ racing within her chest. "Warn me about…?"

Surely he didn't know about the Pill fiasco.

No. How could he? She'd told him she was on them, and he'd obviously believed her. And she had been. She certainly hadn't been lying or trying to pull any kind of funny business.

And if she wound up pregnant…would he still believe her then? That it had just been a fluke?

"Come with me."

She shied back from him as if he was going to grab her hand, which of course he wouldn't. Not here at the hospital.

They did have practice today, so they would have seen each other at some point anyway.

His eyes narrowed as he studied her for a minute, then he simply spun on his heel and walked toward the bank of elevators. Left to her own devices, she followed him, assuming that's what he wanted. He pushed the button for her floor. "You might want to do something about it."

Again her heart skipped a time or two.

Stop it, Tessa. He has no idea that you missed taking your contraceptives.

She didn't ask what he wanted her to do something about, figuring that's why he'd come up to the floor with her. Maybe there was a problem with a patient. Or maybe even the one they'd worked on together. Except he wouldn't be on this floor.

"Is Mr. Phillips okay?"

He glanced back at her. "As far as I know. I haven't checked on him today." He motioned at the desk.

Her eyes skipped across it, seeing the two collection jars.

Wait. The jars. Caren and Holly had mentioned them, and Caren had denied any wrongdoing.

She walked slowly toward the desk, her eyes on the clear glass containers that were now lined with green bills. They were both stuffed almost full.

And then she saw it.

The labels had been changed.

Oh, God.

The simple names the jars had sported before had morphed into hand-drawn likenesses of them. Only these were no ordinary pictures. They'd each been made to look as if they were puckering up. And the jars been turned so the lips met...so she and Clay appeared to be kissing.

Each other.

She made a low sound of distress, and Clay moved to stand beside her. "It's obvious that someone saw us outside the hospital."

"Are they all like this?" she whispered.

"Every single one of them. It isn't Lloyd's doing this time." His breath whistled out in a long pained sigh. "And the worst thing is, we're not the only ones who've seen them."

Since the jars were in an open area on every floor, that stood to reason. "I guess the whole hospital knows about that kiss, then." She groaned, knowing there were going to be endless comments and speculation about what was going on between her and Clay.

And if she suddenly wound up pregnant?

She swallowed hard.

"Yes, the whole hospital knows." He turned to face her. "And so do my mother and Molly."

CHAPTER ELEVEN

Time to do some damage control.

Practice that afternoon had been a bust. Clay hadn't been able to keep his mind on what was happening in the ring, and neither could Tessa, evidently, since Marcos—back in royal form after his hospital stint—had excoriated both of them. Publicly. And had told them to be back tomorrow for a private session.

Everyone else was off the hook.

There'd also been no end to the questions from Clay's mom, who'd believed him when he'd said that Tessa had merely slept over. He'd even let her assume that he'd spent the night on the couch, although he never actually said that he had.

Now she thought he'd lied to her, of all things.

And had warned him about letting himself get too involved, reminding him that they'd already tried that path once and it hadn't worked out. She didn't want to see him get hurt.

He was no longer a little boy, but he was still his mom's son. She was worried about him. And probably with good reason. He'd been shocked by the depth of his response to Tessa the other night. As hard as he'd tried to keep things on an even keel, telling himself that it was all about one night of really good sex, somehow he knew it wasn't. That was as much of a lie as letting his mom believe that he and Tessa had spent a platonic night together.

As if he and Tessa could ever remain platonic.

She drove him insane. And not in a good way.

The worst thing had been when she'd peered a little bit closer at one of the jars and seen the check his mom had made out and slid inside it. It should have grated on him that his parents had voted for Tessa and not for him, but they knew how good she was at *capoeira*. It would be crazy to bet on anyone but her.

Tessa's face had blanched, turning as white as one of the paper sheets the hospital used to cover the exam tables. She hadn't said a word, just backed away from the jars.

He had a feeling her reaction had something to do with that discussion they'd had a couple of weeks ago about his parents paying for her education.

But this wasn't paying for anything. They were simply contributing to a worthy charity.

But Tessa might not have taken it that way.

Clay had been so worked up about his mom getting the wrong idea that he hadn't bothered to see Tessa's reaction as anything other than petulant. But maybe it was more than that.

Tessa was proud. Very much so. Maybe because she hadn't been born here, she felt as if she had more to prove.

But he wasn't a mind reader, neither did he have the time to worry about anything other than the well-being of his daughter. He was not going to drag her through another one of his failures.

Which meant he needed to cool it with Tessa. Big-time.

Only he didn't want to.

He wanted to sleep with her. Again. Despite everything that had gone on with the hospital and with his mom and Molly.

He and Tessa had always been great together in that way. And she was a hot, giving lover who made him reach for the stars. The two of them had had some wild times together.

His body couldn't be blamed for remembering what they'd done and wanting to grab at more of the same. Especially since his love life with Lizza had been lukewarm at best. Once they'd married, she'd tolerated his advances, but beyond that she'd seemed perfectly content to keep to her own side of the bed. The only thing she'd really seemed to like had been when he'd complimented her on an outfit or admired her beauty.

And she was beautiful.

But Tessa had a quality that Lizza could never touch.

A raw, honest sensuality that went to the very core of who she was. And Clay couldn't believe no other man had snatched her up.

Then again, maybe she hadn't wanted to be snatched up. Tessa was so driven to succeed. Maybe that was enough for her.

Except what he'd experienced in his bed said she wanted more.

He ducked into Mr. Phillips's room to check on the man's leg. Brian Perry was there as well, reading the patient's chart. He nodded to the other doctor, who returned the gesture. Tessa had mentioned that the care team had met about his melanoma, and the recommended treatment was a grueling course of chemo. Mr. Phillips had said no.

"How's our patient?" Clay asked. He wouldn't admit that he was disappointed it wasn't Tessa in the room. At least, not to the other doctor.

Mr. Phillips was the one who answered. "I'm ready to go home, that's how I am."

It was said with a smile but, still, he could hear a little note of impatience in the man's voice.

"I'm sure it won't be much longer. But you're going to need to visit a rehab center to get back on your feet. You realize that, don't you?"

"I think I'll skip that, if it's all the same to you, Doc."

Clay looked at the patient's face and saw a

tiredness and grim resignation that made his chest ache.

In the end, it was Mr. Phillips's decision, and Clay had to respect that. "Is your daughter still here?"

The man nodded. "She's going to stay for a while. Her kids are grown, and she said she's wanted to take a vacation for the past year." He shifted on his bed. "I don't think this was quite what she had in mind."

Maybe not, but Clay was glad someone was going to be with him. Maybe she would even talk her dad into moving closer to them.

"I'm sure she's just happy to get to see you for a while." He did a quick check, measuring function in his damaged leg. Dr. Perry stood a few feet back, watching the proceedings without saying anything. Clay assumed he'd already done his own assessment on the site where they'd removed the melanoma. But maybe not.

Once he finished and told Mr. Phillips he'd return tomorrow with news about when he'd be released, he left the room, only to have Brian follow him.

He turned toward the other man. Maybe he'd been right the first time he'd seen Dr. Perry and Tessa doing surgery together. He'd gotten a funny feeling that the other man might like her. Could be that he was going to ask about those damned jars or warn him off.

To which he'd offer a warning of his own: that the man needed to mind his own business. He was in no mood to spare anyone's feelings at the moment.

"You and Tessa know each other from…before, right?"

The question took him by surprise, and yet it was along the lines of what he'd expected. "We knew each other in medical school, yes."

He was not about to admit that he'd been ready to propose to her back then.

"Did she ever express any interest in obstetrics while you were in school?"

His brows came together. "Obstetrics? No. Why?"

Brian leaned against the wall. "I expected her to apply for a fellowship in either cutaneous oncology or Mohs, but Faye Powers mentioned

Tessa had an appointment with her today. When I asked her what it was about, she said she assumed it was about the fellowship positions, since applications are about to start coming in. Faye's still officially the head of the department, at least until she retires next week. She's decided to accept paperwork until they appoint a replacement, although she won't be making the actual decisions about who gets the fellowships."

Brian scuffed a toe on the linoleum. "Tessa did a rotation in Obstetrics, but I didn't think she was headed in that direction."

Clay tried to wrap his head around that.

"Obstetrics? Are you sure?"

The other man shrugged. "I can't think of any other reason Tessa would want to speak with the head of Maternal Fetal medicine, can you?"

"No." Tessa was always full of surprises, but he couldn't imagine her wanting to change specialties midstream. Especially not with her mom's illness driving her in the other direction. But what else could it be?

Something clicked in the back of his head, a few gears engaging the problem.

If she hadn't been on the Pill, he might have wondered if the appointment had anything to do with the night they'd shared together. But she'd assured him she was.

Could she have been so caught up in the moment that she'd lied?

He couldn't imagine her being that irresponsible. Besides, he'd wanted to use a condom, and she'd countered by saying she was on the Pill.

He hadn't argued, accepting the unspoken message—they were both clean, and she was protected.

Brian moved away from the wall. "Well, I thought you might know something. Our department would hate to lose her. She stands to be one of the best we have. I'm already hearing murmurs that the hospital wants to make sure it keeps her."

Clay already knew she was good, but he had no idea why Brian thought he'd know anything about what she was planning.

Those damn collection jars. If his mom thought they were becoming involved again, even knowing their past, everyone at the hospital probably thought the same thing. Or worse. "I'll direct her your way, if the subject comes up." Not that he expected it to.

Except something in him wanted to make sure. *Had* to make sure.

They parted ways, Clay heading down the hallway toward the bank of elevators. The first car opened its doors, and he got in just as the one coming down opened. Tessa emerged from the pack, heading with purpose down the hall toward their patient's room. Putting his hand out, he stopped the elevator doors from closing and murmured his apologies to the other passengers as he stepped off.

"Tess."

His voice stopped her in her tracks, but she didn't turn around right away. When she finally did, her face was pink. What the hell was going on?

"I just checked in on Mr. Phillips, if that's where you're headed. Brian Perry was there, as well." No reason to beat around the bush, but he certainly didn't want to do it standing here in the hall, where anyone could overhear them. "Would you come to my office for a minute? I'd like to talk to you."

He thought she was going to refuse, but then she nodded.

Leading the way, he was careful not to touch her as they got back on the elevator and made their way up to the fifth floor. Neither of them said anything as there were a few other people in the car. Finally they got off and headed down the corridor to Clay's small office. Once inside, he shut the door and motioned her to a seat, while he perched on the front of the desk.

"Like I said, I saw Brian Perry while I was in Mr. Phillips's room."

"Oh?" She looked up at him, clearly confused. "That's what you wanted to talk to me about?"

"In part. He's worried you might be changing specialties."

"Changing specialties? What gave him that idea?"

He crossed one ankle over the other. "Your trip down to the obstetrics department."

Her mouth popped open for several seconds before she closed it again, her teeth sinking into her bottom lip. Then she sat up a little straighter. "I—I'm not sure I follow. Why would he think I was changing specialties?"

She hadn't denied going to Obstetrics. It was more as if she was avoiding the word altogether.

"Maybe because you had an appointment with Dr. Powers, who's collecting fellowship applications until she retires."

Every ounce of color leached from her face. "How did he find out about my appointment?"

"She thought you were applying for a fellowship as well and mentioned it. If Brian Perry knows, others probably do, as well." He leaned forward a bit. "What's going on, Tessa?"

"Nothing." Her voice shook the tiniest bit, belying the word.

His brief moment of suspicion flared back up, finding new fuel and licking at it for all it was worth.

"Does this have anything to do with the other night?" He gripped the edge of his desk with both hands. "We still have *capoeira* practice to contend with, so we're going to have to work to get past this."

"I know. It's just awkward. I don't think either of us expected what happened."

"I certainly didn't expect to hear about you running down to Obstetrics within days of our encounter."

"What do you mean?"

He studied her for a moment or two then decided to be blunt. "You said you were on the Pill. You are, right? Your visit to Faye Powers had nothing to do with our time together."

"Clay, I…" He thought she was going to say something else, but she simply shook her head.

An eerie premonition began to march up his spine. Lizza had gotten pregnant with Molly unexpectedly, and he'd asked her to marry him to make things right. But Tessa hadn't wanted to be married to him back when they'd been dating, and he didn't expect her to want it now. Not that they'd need to.

She's not pregnant.

Time to get that thought out in the open and verify it for his own peace of mind. "Did you take your Pill the night we were together?"

Her hands twisted in front of her. "I—I'd been

so busy over the past week and had several night shifts. By the time I got off… I was exhausted. I should carry them in my purse, but I haven't been involved with…" She shook her head. "The short answer is no, I missed a few days without realizing it. I didn't do it on purpose, Clay, I swear it."

A field of white danced in front of his eyes. He had no doubt she was telling the truth. He could see it in her face. Hear the anguish in her voice.

She might become pregnant. Hell, she might already be. And she'd said nothing.

"That was what your appointment with Faye was about?"

"Yes."

She wanted to know what her options were. They ran through his head. Start back on the Pill and hope for the best. Morning-after pill. Abortion. Adoption.

Each of those made his gut churn and his throat tighten. But it wasn't up to him. Although he damn well would have liked some kind of say in the matter. "What did Faye say?"

"She said since I missed several doses at this point…"

Her words trailed away.

A few tense muscles relaxed. Did that mean she hadn't gone back on the Pill?

"What about Plan B?"

Her brows came together. "I'm right at the limit for time. I need to do it now, if I'm going to."

Something made him lean forward. "Don't take it, Tess." In that moment a crash of realization had him off the desk and reaching for her, hauling her out of the seat and into his arms. He loved her. Had never really stopped loving her.

She wrapped her arms around his neck, unaware of the thoughts veering around inside his head. "I don't know what to do. Please, believe me, Clay. I never meant this to happen. Any of it. Not that it has."

"I know." He pulled her tight against him, memories of the other night chasing him down a fast-moving stream. One he couldn't seem to get out of. Tipping her head back, he kissed her. And just like that, things exploded between them. Mouths sealing together, hands traveling over each other's bodies in a mixture of anguish and desperation.

Clay turned with her still in his arms and pressed her against the desk, not even attempting to hide what she did to him. He pulled his mouth free. "Say yes."

He had no idea what he was asking for. Say yes to having sex with him in his office? Say yes to having his baby? He didn't care. He just wanted to hear the word.

Her hands went to the back of his head. "Yes," she whispered, just before she hauled him back to her.

Holding her against him with one hand, he swept papers and a pencil cup onto the floor and lifted her onto the desk. She leaned back, her light blue scrubs the only thing stopping him from finishing the job. He would soon remedy that. But first no more misunderstandings. "Stay right there."

He grabbed his wallet out of one of the desk drawers and removed a condom. If she wasn't already pregnant, he sure as hell wasn't going to purposely try to make it come true. No matter what his heart was saying.

He pushed down the front of his own navy

scrubs, sure there had to be some kind of rule against attendings having sex with residents, but he and Tessa weren't just any mismatched pair. They had history. One that had repeated itself a few days ago.

Ripping open the condom, he frowned when Tessa sat up.

Rather than leaping off his desk and hightailing it out of his office, she simply took the packet from his hand and set it on the desk. "I know we have to hurry, but give me a second."

She palmed him, her eyes closing as she gently squeezed then trailed her fingertips down the underside and slowly back up to encircle him again.

His breath hissed in his lungs. Yes. This felt so right. So good.

Before he could move to stop her, Tessa slid off the desk and knelt in front of him, her lips sliding down the side of his erection in a slow, languorous journey. Then she came back the way she'd gone, opening her mouth and taking him inside. Yellow lights flashed in his head at the bevy of sensations that crawled over every part of him, threatening him with imminent meltdown.

Pushing his fingers deep into her hair and closing around the silky strands, he allowed himself the luxury of closing his eyes and pumping into her heat, once, twice, before slowly pulling free. He sucked down a couple of breaths then reached to bring her back to her feet. It had to be now or he wouldn't find the strength to stop.

Setting her back on the desk once again, he eased her back in an act of reverence this time rather than a rush toward completion. Her arms curled above her head, eyes on his as he reached for the condom and rolled it down himself. He wrapped his hands around the backs of her knees and tugged her toward the edge of the desk, her hair fanning behind her. Rather than wait for him to pull the bottoms of her scrubs off, she rolled over until she was on her stomach then pushed the garment down her hips, baring her luscious bottom to his view. A much more practical—and quick—solution than getting undressed all the way.

"You sure?" he gritted.

She wiggled her ass. "Does it look like I'm sure?"

Leaning down to nip her neck and trail his lips

up to her ear, capturing it between his teeth, he muttered, "Tell me you want me, then."

"I want you."

With that he found her, amazed that she was already moist and ready against his tip. With a hard push he entered her, going deep and holding himself there while he absorbed the tightness of the fit—the heat he could feel even through the protective barrier.

Her muttered *"Meu Deus"* in her native tongue said the feeling was mutual.

Gripping her wrists, he moved them above her head and held them there with one hand as he began to thrust inside her. Lord, she fired him up as no other woman ever had, bringing him immediately to the brink of release whenever he touched her.

He slid the fingers of his other hand beneath her right hip as he continued to press deep, finding that sensitive little bud between her legs and stroking gently. He wasn't going to be able to hold on for long, no matter what he did.

It didn't look as if it was going to matter, because Tessa began moving her hips as he continued to manipulate and squeeze, hoping he could at least hold on long enough for her to…

Just then, she pushed up against him in a couple of hard, fast thrusts and went off with a raw whimper that reached deep inside him and set him free. He came in a series of disjointed bursts that only slowed when the hands he still held went lax.

He leaned down and kissed her neck, allowing his tongue to travel up it.

It evidently tickled, because she squirmed, letting out a strangled laugh. "Clay, I need to get up."

Aware that he might be crushing her, he hurriedly stood, pulling out of her and wincing when he immediately missed the contact.

He removed the condom, aware of her scent clinging to his body, despite the fact that he'd been mostly covered in clothes.

Tessa was slower to move and he couldn't help but admire the view, his hands itching to cup her butt and absorb the firm softness—two words that should have been at odds with one another but somehow weren't.

When she finally did get to her feet and pulled her panties—black lace, he noted—and scrubs back into place, she turned toward him with a smile. "I certainly didn't see that in the residency tips manual."

He relaxed, surprised at how tense he'd been a second ago.

"Didn't you?" He smiled back. "I'm sure I saw it listed somewhere in there. Maybe in the FAQs."

She came over and lifted her hands to his face, rubbing her thumbs along his cheeks. "Thank you for not freaking out about everything. I'm sure it'll be fine."

Oh, he was freaked out, all right. He was just good at hiding certain things. Sometimes even from himself. Surely they could work something out. Especially now.

"What did Dr. Powers say about the festival—about training? Did you ask her?"

"We don't even know if I'm pregnant yet, but she said there shouldn't be any problem as I've been doing the workouts for years. Sitting at home and doing nothing would be the worst thing

I could do. I just need to make sure my core temperature doesn't climb too high."

"Good to hear. And if you do end up pregnant—" he leaned against the desk "—we'll figure something out. I can help with expenses—"

"No." The hands on his face went still and then fell to her sides as she backed up, her smile fading in a second.

"Tessa…" His patience dried up just as fast. "I'm not asking. I'm telling."

"Excuse me?" Her eyes turned to frost. "If I am pregnant—and *if* I decide to keep it—I can take care of the baby on my own. With no help from anyone. Not you. Not your parents."

A reference to them paying her tuition? That was just damned ridiculous. That was years ago, and Tessa had done a great job proving she could do a lot of things. But taking care of a baby while tackling the crazy hours that went along with residency? Why would she, when people were willing to pitch in and lend a hand? Besides, it was *his* baby, too. And his parents would want to know that they were about to become grandparents again.

"Why are you being so stubborn? You're still doing your residency, for God's sake." He tried for a more conciliatory tone. "Let's meet for dinner and talk about this."

"I've said all I'm going to say." She ran her fingers through her hair, no longer looking directly at him. "I won't keep the baby from you, if there ends up being a baby. But I don't want any financial help." This time she did look at him. "Please, Clay."

Anger washed over him, reminding him of all those fights they'd had in the past. Nothing had changed. She was still as unreasonable as ever. He put his hands up. "Have it your way. I guess I'll see you at practice this afternoon."

"I guess you will."

With that she opened the door to his office and strode out with an air of confidence. As if she hadn't just been sprawled across his desk.

He slowly walked around and picked up the items he'd scattered in his haste to have her, shaking his head. She might not be willing to let him help her but that didn't mean he had to listen to her.

And if he couldn't help her directly, he could always help their child, if there was one.

Surely she wouldn't stop him from assuring himself the baby had the chance for a bright future.

He plunked the pencil cup back onto his desk and sat down to come up with a plan.

One not even Tessa could refuse.

CHAPTER TWELVE

SHE COULDN'T CONCENTRATE.

No matter what she did, Tessa couldn't seem to get the upper hand on Clay during practice. They'd come to a kind of uneasy truce over the past week and a half, coming to practice and performing in a way that even Marcos seemed happy with.

Only not today.

Because her period was late. It was to be expected that her system would be messed up, as she'd stopped taking the Pill, so one day was no national tragedy. But she couldn't shake the feeling there might be another reason behind it.

If so, what was she going to do? Neither of them had spoken about the issue since that day in his office, and they certainly hadn't slept together again. But there was a nagging sense of disquiet inside her. If she was pregnant, she was going to have to let him know. It was only right. He was bound to find out, even if she tried to hide it from him. And then all hell would break loose.

And rightfully so.

She'd told him she wouldn't try to keep the baby from him, and she wouldn't.

But what that would entail she had no idea. She didn't want him to start back up with the gifts… with always needing to take care of her.

She misjudged a jump and slid sideways, falling to the mat. For the third time today.

"Tessita." Marcos clucked his tongue. "What is wrong?"

"Nothing." Her voice came out a little too shrill, making both the studio head and Clay look sharply at her. Hell. If she kept this up, she might as well hold up a sign and let everyone know: *I missed my period, and I'm terrified.*

Clay touched her arm. "You okay?"

The words were said with such compassion that her eyes stung. Blinking quickly to rid them of the sensation, she went back into the "ready" stance. "I'm fine. Let's try it again."

"I think maybe that's enough."

And so it began. "Clay, I said I'm fine."

Everyone else in the studio had already finished, and Marcos had sent them home so he could work with just the two of them. So there was no beat to drive her forward, no supportive murmurs from the circle of participants to help center her.

Just keep telling yourself that, Tessa. You know it has nothing to do with that.

Maybe she should let Clay help her. Not financially, but emotionally. There was nothing smothering about that. If she was pregnant, Molly would be this child's half sister. And Megan and Frank Matthews would certainly want to see the baby from time to time. It was selfish to think she could cut Clay's parents out altogether.

And her own dad would want to help, as well. They both had busy schedules, but that could change. This would force them all to slow down. To rely on each other.

It wasn't charity. It was a village raising a child. Wasn't that the right way to go about it? She had to believe it was.

Yes. She would talk to him about it after their session was over. *Abre a mão*—open her hand—as Brazilians liked to say and compromise just a little bit.

As long as he didn't go overboard, they should be fine.

She might not even be pregnant.

Yes, but shouldn't she be prepared if the possibility arose?

"Ready?" she asked him.

He nodded. "If we're going to do it, let's do it."

This time, when she swerved, Clay matched her, move for move, step for step. It was the best session they'd had the whole time they'd practiced.

Fifteen minutes later, Marcos called time and gave her a quick hug, handing her a towel. "*Perfeito.* I don't know what that last part was all about, but do not change one thing before next week. I'm counting on both of you to put on a good show. One as good as you just did. Can you do that?"

Her eyes clipped Clay's and smiled when he

nodded. "Cross your fingers, Marcos. Because that's as good as it's going to get."

"That's as good as I need it to be." He tossed Clay a towel, as well. "I'm going to lock up and make sure everything's secure before I leave. I'll see you at our last practice."

The second Marcos was out of earshot Clay turned to her. "You're late, aren't you?"

Her eyes widened, although she should have realized he would figure out why she was off her game. "Yes, but only by a day. That could be because my hormones are out of whack."

"Possibly."

He didn't look convinced and suddenly Tessa wanted to make sure things were okay between them. She hadn't done that during their breakup and it was something she'd regretted…not really talking to him about things. Touching his arm, she said, "I'm so sorry for making a mess of this. If I'd just let you use protection—"

His mouth went up into a half smile. "You're not the only one to blame. You didn't expect me to keep you at my house and ply you with wine and kisses."

"I don't remember the wine, but I definitely remember the rest of it."

Linking his fingers with hers, he gave her hand a squeeze. "It'll be okay, Tess. No matter what happens."

He truly believed that. That fact filled her with hope. Maybe it *would* be okay. "Will Molly be upset if I do end up being pregnant?"

"I think she'll be thrilled. Especially if you give us a chance to be involved in the baby's life."

She glanced back to make sure Marcos wasn't coming and nodded toward the front door. She wanted to drop a bombshell and see what happened. *Open your hand, Tessa, abre a mão.*

Once they were outside, she turned to him. "You talked about wanting to help." She licked her lips. "If it comes down to it, I think I'm going to need it. I can't expect my dad to shoulder everything on his own."

"Of course. I already said I'd—"

"I don't want money. I'd just like the baby to have a support system. And to know his or her sister."

He touched her face. "You won't regret it, honey. I promise."

Leaning into his touch, she tried to make herself believe that it was all going to be okay, just as he'd said. Because she'd made her decision, even if she hadn't voiced it yet. She was keeping the baby, if there was one. She just had to figure out how to have a child and still reach for her own dreams.

Letting someone help didn't have to mean being a charity case. She would keep telling herself that. There was a world of difference between bags of used clothes and a new life that needed to be nurtured and loved. This was her way of starting down that road.

Clay's thumb curved under her jaw. "Molly's with me tonight, or I'd ask you to come home with me."

"It's okay." She thought for a minute or two. "How would you feel about the three of us doing something together?"

"You, me and Molly?"

Tessa nodded.

"I think Molly would be thrilled. Are you sure?"

"Yes. A close friend just left for a medical mission, and I'm feeling a little lost these days. Although I think she's the one who changed the labels on those collection jars."

"I told you you had some loyal fans. Okay, let me call Mom and let her know we're on our way."

Tessa hesitated. "Will this make things awkward with your mother?"

"She loves you, Tessa. Nothing will ever change that."

Warmth bloomed inside her that spread to every square inch of her being. "I was pretty awful when we broke up."

He shrugged. "I never told her most of what happened. Just that we decided it wasn't right. And if things change, she'll be over the moon."

"You're a good man, Clayton Matthews."

"Maybe not so good, because right now I'm wishing that Molly was spending the night with my mom."

She wrapped her hand around his upper arm as they crossed the street and made their way down the sidewalk. Traffic rushed by at a frenetic pace, a harsh reminder of what they shouldn't do. "Let's not be in a hurry, Clay. We'll just take everything slow and see what happens."

"I'm up for that." He dropped a kiss on top of her head.

Maybe time had dulled the pain of the past. She didn't want to get her hopes up or think that they could go back to what they'd been before. But maybe they could forge something... friendship, or even a little more out of the ashes of the past.

She'd never really gotten over him, she could admit that to herself now. It still didn't mean they should go back in time or start dating again.

Dating?

Hadn't they already gone light years beyond that? They'd made love more than once at his house and again at the hospital. There was evidently something still sizzling on the burner between them. And maybe those sparks had created a tiny new human. She didn't know yet. But within the next couple of weeks Tessa was sure they'd have their answer. Whether they were ready or not.

* * *

"Me next!" Molly watched Tessa go down the plastic slide at Family World and clapped her hands in glee.

Clay wouldn't have believed Tessa had this in her, but the kids' outdoor park and eatery had been her suggestion. And she'd claimed it had been one of her favorite places to go as a child. Bright stadium lights illuminated the place as if it were still daytime.

Molly seemed to like it, that was for sure. She'd barely let go of Tessa's hand long enough to try any of the rides herself, so Tessa had been forced to go with her on most of them. Which was fine by Clay. Something about seeing the pair of them together gave him a taste of what it would be like to see her with their child—and created a funny little ache in his chest that was getting harder and harder to ignore.

It was strange how he'd gone from "if" there was a child to hoping there was one. Tessa would be nothing like Lizza. She put her heart and soul into people...not into things. It was probably one of the reasons she'd wanted to become a doctor so very badly.

And the fact that he hadn't needed to finagle his schedule around to be with her only added to the enjoyment of spending time together. It seemed as if they were on the verge of the break-through that had eluded them during their years together.

But he would take it slow, just as she'd asked.

Tessa laughed as Molly tugged her toward the next attraction, a huge trampoline area, sectioned into large rectangles so multiple people could bounce at one time. The whole thing was then surrounded by a net and rubber bumpers.

"Wait." He slowed her with a touch to the arm. "You're not going on there, are you?"

"It's fine. Dr. Powers said I could follow my normal routine."

"That looks normal to you?"

"Absolutely." She gave him a smile and a wave and got in line with Molly, leaving him to head up to the elevated viewing area.

The attraction was busy, and they had to wait until two people exited before they could go in.

Then they were climbing up the stairs and onto the taut canvas surface toward the available rectangles. Holding Molly's hands when they reached the first one, Tessa bounced up and down and side to side, the woman's hips swinging as the pair did some goofy things.

Goofy to his insides, as well.

Then Tessa moved to the other free rectangle, while Molly continued to jump in the one they'd just shared. To his surprise, Tessa did a test backflip, landing right on her feet. His daughter stopped to watch, eyes wide as she proceeded to execute a series of moves that would have made Marcos proud. She added twists and rolls and *capoeira* moves that became even more impressive when performed on the elastic surface. Within a minute or two a small crowd had formed in the viewing area, but Tessa was oblivious, the concentration on her face blocking out everything but Molly and what she was doing for the little girl.

In a flurry that reminded him of the last few moments of a fireworks display, when the operators let loose everything they had left at their disposal, Tessa went into a series of arcing jumps that moved closer and closer to the dividing line where Molly was standing, her little body bouncing in glee, her laughs echoing, as with one final leap that ended in a forward roll, Tessa stopped right at the edge of her canvas, facing his daughter.

Murmurs went up from those watching and someone whistled. Tessa glanced to the side, blinking in apparent shock. But she quickly recovered and, holding Molly's hand, directed the girl to give a little bow along with her.

His chest swelled with pride. Hell, he loved that woman. If he could only get her to see how good they could be together. How good they *were* together.

They could be so much more.

Their romance from years past had been a whirlwind affair, seeming much like that blast of moves she'd just performed on the trampoline. This time around he had to respect her wishes to go slow, focusing on steady progress that didn't scare her or make her want to bolt.

Only Clay had no idea how to do any of that.

Maybe he shouldn't try to plan it. He could just take things one day at a time. One moment at a time, starting with getting through the festival… seeing if she was pregnant or if all of this was a false alarm. And if it was? Would he still want to move forward?

Tessa stepped onto the ladder, making sure Molly was the first one on the ground. She paused to shake the operator's hand with a smile.

Oh, yes. He wanted to move forward.

The crowd dissipated, and when he joined Tessa he found her holding his daughter's hand, her cheeks flushed with exertion and enthusiasm. The woman was gorgeous.

And he couldn't help but lean forward and give her a quick kiss on the lips.

Her eyes registered shock but she didn't pull away and his daughter seemed to take the move in stride, the way kids did, already talking about what to do next.

"I think I need to take a few minutes to rest, if that's okay," Tessa said.

"Are you okay?"

She rolled her eyes. "I'm fine. Just tired."

Molly nodded. "Me, too. Maybe we can get a corn dog or something."

The rest of the evening went better than he could have planned and when he dropped her off at the brownstone where she lived, this time it was Tessa who leaned over and kissed his cheek. "See you at work tomorrow, handsome."

His throat tightened as a wave of emotion swept over him. The old endearment had seemed to flow from her lips with almost no effort at all. He forced a smile that he hoped looked more casual than he felt and tweaked her nose. "See you."

"Well, Mr. Phillips, I guess this is goodbye."

The elderly patient sat in a wheelchair flanked by a nurse's aide, Tessa and Clay as they waited for his daughter to bring the car around. He'd stuck by his decision not to undergo chemotherapy, saying that at his age he just wanted to enjoy the days he had left. Tessa couldn't blame him, but all the same she wished there was something more that could be done.

Sometimes there wasn't, and you just had to acknowledge that fact. It didn't make it any easier to accept, and she couldn't imagine a time when she wouldn't feel that crushing blow when a patient's cancer was discovered too late. But at least Mr. Phillips had lived a full life, unlike her mom. He was ready to go and would be surrounded by loving family members. His daughter had even convinced him to consider selling his house and moving back west with her.

"Thank you for being a straight shooter." He held out his hand, and she shook it, giving it a gentle squeeze. This would probably be the last time she ever saw him. And that was hard.

Clay came forward and also shook his hand. "Make sure you continue doing the exercises they showed you. You want to maintain as much mobility as possible in that leg."

She realized that somehow Clay had learned the art of compartmentalizing, dealing with the things he was able to fix and pushing aside those things he couldn't.

Not a bad trait for her to learn, as well.

Like maybe putting their past mistakes in a compartment and leaving them there? Allow-

ing what was here and now to be what she focused on?

Surely they'd both learned from what had happened. She knew she had. At least she hoped that
was true.

Mr. Phillips's daughter pulled up and Clay
helped their patient move from the wheelchair
into the front seat of the vehicle. Then the door
closed, and he was waving goodbye through the
glass of the window.

Goodbye, dear soul.

She closed her eyes for a second or two and
felt a hand touch hers. Just enough for her to
know it was Clay and that he was lending her
support.

Taking a deep breath, she opened her eyes and
smiled up at him, noting the nurse's aide had already taken the wheelchair back inside, leaving
them alone on the sidewalk as the van pulled
away.

He moved to stand in front of her. "I know you
asked me not to put in a good word for you with
Josiah Wesley. Would you reconsider that? He
has several residents interested in applying for a

fellowship, and I want to make sure you're in a good position to get one of the spots."

Don't overreact, Tess. Stop and think for a second.

Before she could, Clay went on, "I know you can do it on your own, but most applicants are going to have a list of references. I'm simply asking to be one of yours."

That made her blink. When he put it like that, it sounded much more reasonable. And she knew Dr. Wesley's reputation well enough that she was sure he wouldn't hand her a fellowship based solely on Clay's word, friend or not. She'd done all the hard work in getting ready and making sure she was up to speed on the newest techniques. Clay was just acting as a reference. And he knew her better than almost anyone, despite their rocky past. He knew her character. And that's what a reference was all about.

So she nodded. "Thank you. I'd appreciate that." The relief on his face was almost comical, and it made her smile once again. "Am I that hard to get along with?"

"No. But you are that proud. And I don't mind

telling you I'm damned impressed by everything you've accomplished."

"Thanks. I'm getting off in a few minutes. When does your shift end?"

"Same time, actually." He hesitated. "Mom is watching Molly at my apartment today, though, or I'd ask you to come back for dinner."

"My place is free."

"I thought you had three other people living there."

She laughed. "I do, but Caren has already left for her mission, remember? So that leaves two. And I think the only one off today is Sam. So if we tiptoe past his door, we might be able to sneak in unseen."

His finger hooked around hers. "But what about all that noise you'll be making."

"Wow, that sure of yourself, are you?"

"No. That sure of you."

Her brows went up. "Oh, now you've just throw down a gauntlet I can't resist. I bet you tickets to the ball game of your choice that I'm as quiet as a church mouse."

"You're on, Tess. But just in case, I think you'd better turn the speakers on your MP3 player way up."

Tessa fell back onto the bed, her breath heaving from her lungs, the strains of jazz still blaring in the room. She laid a hand on her bare stomach and stared up at the ceiling, trying to get her racing heart back under control. "Okay, so maybe the church mice were throwing a party today."

Clay rolled onto his stomach and bracketed his arms on either side of her shoulders. "That must have been some party, with all that shouting they were doing."

"God. You don't think Sam heard anything, do you?"

"Does it matter if he did?"

She punched him in the chest. "Only if I want to be able to look him in the face again."

"He didn't see me come in. He'll probably assume it was a show on TV."

"Jazz punctuated by moments of moaning and crying. I see how that could become a whole new trend."

Gripping her waist, he flipped back over, dragging her on top of him. "Don't knock it until you try it."

"I just did."

"And did you like it?"

She slid up his body until she was perched on a certain part of him. "So much that I'm thinking about repeating the experience."

"Hell, woman, you're going to kill me."

Only it didn't feel as if she was killing him. In fact, if what was happening beneath her was any indication, she'd say that he was up to the challenge.

Forty minutes later, dressed back in her street clothes, she headed out to the kitchen to get them both a glass of wine. Stuck beneath a magnet on the door of the huge stainless-steel refrigerator was a note penned in a decidedly masculine hand.

Interesting choice in music. Headed to the hospital, so don't bother sneaking him out.

She grabbed the note and scrunched her nose. *Gads! And you can't have wine, ninny. You still haven't had your period.*

Another little something she was going to have to deal with at some point.

Making her way back to her unit with one glass of wine and one bottle of water, she was slightly disappointed that Clay had also gotten dressed while she'd been getting their drinks. She set them on the scarf across her dresser and waved the note under his nose. "I blame this on you. You can't get me all sexed up like that in front of people."

He glanced at the words then wrapped his hands around her waist and reeled her in. "It was hardly in front of him. But if that's the kind of thing you like…"

"Stop it. I'm already going to have a hard time not turning beet red the next time I see him."

"I'd like to be there to see that." He glanced at the drinks with a slight frown. "It's been almost a week. And since we just had sex, I'm assuming you still haven't seen any sign of activity."

"Not that kind of activity, no." She pulled away and sat on the bed. "My emotions are all mixed up about it right now."

"So you're still planning on keeping it?"

"That's the plan." But beyond that she had no idea what she was going to do.

He uncapped the water bottle and handed it to her then took a big sip of his wine before sitting down next to her. He slid his hand across her belly, sending a shiver through her. "I don't mind telling you, I'm already starting to think of this as a reality."

Pressing his hand against her, she linked fingers with him. "This isn't at all what I'd planned on. But now that it might be a possibility…" She shrugged. "A million things have been going through my head, like names and whether it might be a boy or a girl."

"A girl." He leaned over and kissed her temple. "One who has red hair and is as proud as her mama."

"Or a boy, with a big heart like his daddy."

Clay's thumb rubbed across her stomach. "I want to talk to you about something."

Everything in her tensed up. *Please, don't ask me to marry you, Clay. Not like this. Not for this reason.*

She was being stupid. Of course he wasn't

going to do that. They didn't even know for sure if she was pregnant. And he had a daughter of his own to think about.

"Okay, what is it?"

He didn't look at her or get down on one knee, so a part of her relaxed.

"I know it's still early and this could all be a false alarm, but I've been thinking. You don't want any financial support, right?"

Her jaw tightened. "We've already been over this."

"And I'm willing to respect that. But this baby will be mine as well, and I want to make sure he or she is provided for. What if I set up a college fund that would be used just by the child?"

Tessa's heart turned to ice in her chest. "You mean pay for everything? Kind of like your parents did for me?"

She hadn't meant the words to come out with the harsh edge they had, but there was no way she could call them back now. Not when all the walls she'd just let down started to go back up, block by block. She knew him well enough to know that he would just keep pushing, trying different angles in order to get his way. *She* wouldn't accept his financial help, so he would just bypass her and give it to their child instead.

Was that what she wanted? For herself? For the baby?

As if sensing her thoughts, Clay pulled his hand from her stomach and stared straight ahead. Then he took a drink of his wine. Then another.

He stood to his feet and set the glass back on the dresser.

Just when she thought he was going to leave without saying another word, he turned to her. "If you think I'm just going to sit back and not participate in my child's life, you're wrong, Tessa. You can't expect me to help Molly get an education someday and do nothing for this child."

"But it's different with Molly—"

"No. It's not." He sent her an angry glare. "Even if she lived with her mother on a full-time basis, I would still want to contribute—to have some say—in what happens to her. It's the same for any child you and I might have. I would want to take care of him or her. How can you not see that?"

I want to take care of him or her.

At those words, all the anger from the past bubbled out of the compartment she'd built for it and tainted everything they'd shared over the past couple of weeks. His constant need to take care of her years ago—to give her things—had become a point of friction, rubbing at her until she was raw. Well, she could read the writing on the wall. He was about to start doing it all over again, and if she gave in on this point he would start pressing her to give in on other areas.

"That's not your choice to make, though. I think I'm perfectly capable of taking care of myself and any child I might have."

His face closed, turning to stone. "That might be true, but you can't stop me from setting up a fund like the one I have for Molly. Neither can you stop the child from using it once he or she comes of legal age."

Horror went through her. Would he actually go against her wishes like that?

"Don't draw this line, Clay. Please." All her hopes for making things work between them shriveled in an instant. Nothing had changed. Nothing.

"I'm not the one drawing the line. You are. And if you think I won't step over it, you're wrong. I just did."

With that, Clay picked up his wallet from the nightstand and shoved it in his back pocket. Out came his car keys. And without another look in her direction he let himself out of the door and, very probably, out of her life.

CHAPTER THIRTEEN

TESSA STOOD IN the circle of *capoeiristas* without a partner.

Clay had not shown up for practice. Not that she could blame him after the bitter words they'd hurled at each other. Fifteen minutes had gone by and Marcos was beyond frantic.

"What did you say to him?"

Her? Why did he assume she was to blame?

Maybe because she was. She'd reacted badly to Clay's words, throwing them away before she'd had time to sift through them rationally.

Of course he'd want to provide for any child he had. For her to expect that he'd be hands-on with everything except his money was ridiculous. But she wasn't exactly sure how to fix it. Or even if she should.

It could be this was the confirmation she

needed that she and Clay were never meant to be together.

Except the problem had always been much more on her side than on his. He was a caring, generous man. He always had been. And she'd hurled it back in his face time and time again.

Over two bags of hand-me-down clothes?

People all over the world would have been happy to have gotten those clothes. So why not her? Did she see herself as so much better than everyone else?

Hadn't she gathered her own bags of clothes over the years and put them in the receptacle of a homeless shelter just down the road?

Yes. She had.

But right now she had more immediate issues to think about. Like what she was going to do about the match. It was possible she'd just ruined things for everyone, including all those people at the hospital who were expecting to see her go head to head with Clay.

Well, she already had.

And she'd come out the loser.

Maybe it was time to change that. She wasn't sure how. But she'd figure it out after this practice.

"I don't know where he is, but we should come up with a plan B, just in case."

She cringed, realizing that was the common name for the morning-after pill. The one she'd thought about taking after their first night together.

Only she hadn't been able to bring herself to do it.

Marcos let out a long wounded sigh and let off a string of Portuguese words that probably had his mother rolling over in her grave. "I'll be your partner. It's the only way."

But if Clay didn't show up, Marcos was holding her personally responsible. He'd left the words unsaid, but it didn't take a rocket scientist to hear the subtext coming through loud and clear. She had no doubt he would try to call Clay after they were done tonight.

That thought made her stomach churn.

They went through the motions, and they were

actually better partners than she and Clay had ever been, since they were closer in skill level. But she knew right away that the fire and passion that had punctuated her sessions with Clay were missing. Marcos did his best to cover for her, but her moves were lifeless caricatures of what good *capoeira* should look like. Even the people keeping time with the drum and instruments seemed to sense it and it came through in their playing.

If this match was ruined, it was her fault.

Unless she did something about it.

But what?

The idea came to her just as Marcos made his next move. She spun away, the energy she'd been looking for coming back with a vengeance.

It had worked once before, maybe it would work again. At least she could try.

This might be her only chance to fix the mistakes of the past—and of the present. With a little luck and a whole lot of praying.

She just hoped it worked.

It had taken Tessa two days to get up the courage to send out the gold-foiled invitation. And she'd gotten no response. At all. As the week before the festival went by in a whirlwind of activity and patients, Tessa's days began to run together in an endless stream, punctuated by a definite lack of sleep.

No word on whether Clay had even received her request. All she could do was hope he'd remember the invitation she'd sent at the beginning of their relationship and see this for the olive branch it was.

She loved the man, she now realized. Wanted a second chance.

Only the festival was here, and time had run out.

As she changed into her white outfit and cinched the purple and green *capoeira* cord around her waist, she wondered if he'd *ever* forgive her for being so intractable and arrogant.

And if he didn't? What did she do then?

She had no idea. And a tiny wave of nausea had hit her this morning, similar to the one she'd felt during practice the other night. It hadn't lasted long, and at first she'd attributed it to nerves over the match today and what had happened with

Clay. But now she wasn't so sure. Her period was still nowhere to be seen, and her doubts about everything turning out okay were growing by the second.

Marcos, already suited up and ready, came back to the dressing area and found her. *"Pronta?"*

"I don't know. I've never had to do the top match before." During their other demonstrations her spot had always been tucked somewhere in the middle.

Her old friend laid a hand on her arm. "It's not going to be any different, *querida*. You'll be surrounded by friends, enclosed in our circle." He moved on to more practical issues. "The match area has been moved down the hill a bit so that people will be able to see into the circle."

"Okay." She took a couple of deep breaths and then blew them back out. "Do you want to run through anything before we go out there? Practice?"

One of the other players came over to where they were standing, and Marcos held up a finger to tell him to wait. "We're not going to practice any more. We don't need to."

Since when did the *capoeira* master not want to practice? Never, that Tessa could remember. Maybe he was responding to her nerves and didn't want to make them worse. Or maybe he was worried about his epilepsy showing up again. He hadn't said anything about that attack, and Tessa had gotten the feeling he didn't want to talk about it.

He tapped her under the chin. "I'll see you over on the field in ten minutes."

"Okay."

His epilepsy wasn't the only thing Marcos had failed to mention. He hadn't talked about Clay, either, so she guessed he hadn't called to confront him after all. What was going to happen with all those collection cups? Or to Clay's job, for that matter, since they'd given the administrator their word that they'd put on this match? And the hospital trustees had approved matching the money in the winning jar.

Well, she and Clay had tried. And it hadn't worked out any better this time than it had the last time.

All because of her.

She checked her appearance once more before walking out of the space and down the hill, following other members of the *capoeira* studio as they grouped by the staging area.

Trying to shake the nervous energy from her hands by wiggling them at her sides, she joined the *roda* of participants as they waited for the signal that would send the first pair into the ring. She and Clay were supposed to be the last to perform, the whole exhibition taking about thirty minutes. She glanced around the area. Spectators were already starting to gather in the designated spot, which was just as Marcos had said, high enough that they'd be able to see into the circle. It really was a smart move on his part, because the action would be hard to see otherwise.

She caught sight of her housemates standing together at the front of the crowd. She sent them a quick wave. Caren had already gone, but Holly and Sam were there, along with a woman she didn't recognize. She tilted her head. Was that Kimberlyn? She *was* supposed to arrive today, and from the picture that Caren had left of her… yes, she thought it might be. It was nice of her to come out, although, knowing Holly, she probably hadn't had much of a choice. She made a note to herself to help the new arrival get settled in.

Marcos caught her eye and gave a slight nod.

They were ready to start.

The tambourines began setting up the basic rhythm, while the third man with a long curved *berimbau* added the deeper bass notes, using the single string stretched from end to end along with the *shoop-shoop* made by pebbles in the gourd at the base of the instrument. A minute went by while everyone absorbed the acoustics and then joined in with claps and a lilting chant they used for every match. Soon Tessa would feel the kind of euphoric state that drove the participants forward. It was all natural, powerful and earthy.

The first two *capoeiristas* entered the ring, their sinuous weaving steps carrying them forward and back, arms sweeping in wide arcs that carried their whole bodies along with them. Each bout was programmed to last two minutes, except for Tessa's, which was fifteen, so they didn't have much time to demonstrate their skill. The pair was doing a phenomenal job, however, both going into joint handstands, their legs bent at the knees, bodies perfectly still for several beats before coming back down at the same time.

They transitioned smoothly into their next group of moves, their cords swinging at their waists. Each pair of fighters had been geared to highlight different skill sets, moving from beginners and going up the ranks to advanced—with like cord colors entering the *roda* together.

Tessa and Clay were to have been the exception. Her cord was two steps below Marcos's, so they were closer in skill than she and Clay.

Not that it mattered. Her heart ached as pairs of *capoeiristas* entered and exited the circle, getting closer and closer to her turn.

There was nothing to do but go through with it and act as if it was all part of the plan. Then afterward?

Well, first she was going to have a good cry. All by herself.

Next, she was going to hunt down Clayton Matthews and plead her case in person. Maybe sending an invitation hadn't been such a good idea. Men didn't take hints, right? Well, she would just have to be more direct the next time around: she would accept whatever help he wanted to give her.

The second to last participants entered the ring, and Tessa tried to get herself to a place where she could concentrate on what needed to be done. When she went to catch Marcos's eye, she was surprised to find him looking elsewhere. She frowned, continuing to sing along with the rest of the group. Normally the pair would make eye contact and prepare to go forward.

Something was wrong. His epilepsy?

Her nerves went on high alert, trying to figure out what she should do. She really didn't want to enter that ring alone and go through a series of moves that had no purpose except to show off. One partner fed off the give and take of the other.

And if Marcos was sick, she wanted to be there to help take care of him.

Just as Clay had wanted to be there for her. For the baby. God, she'd made such a phenomenal mess of things.

The participants currently in the ring were

slowly backing toward their spots, the signal for her and Marcos to move forward.

She had to do it. She'd given her word. Maybe he'd arranged for one of the other members of the studio to take his spot. If so, she'd soon find out.

Stepping forward with the low ducking side steps that kept to a strict beat, she glanced again to see that Marcos hadn't budged from his spot at the perimeter of the ring.

What was going on?

Then someone moved just beyond the edge of the *roda*, and the group parted to let whoever it was pass.

Her heart stopped in her chest, and for a second she thought she might fall to the ground. It was Clay. He was dressed in his white *capoeira* gear, his yellow cord knotted at the side of his waist. And he was moving toward her in those familiar crouching strides.

Tears formed in her eyes, making it hard to focus for a second. She blinked them away, sure she was seeing things.

But Clay was still there, passing to her side, leaning to and fro as he did, reminding her of a cobra. Only his eyes didn't have the dead look of a snake. They looked alive and warm and…

"Got your invitation," he said, just as he slid past again.

He had! And he was here.

She arched her spine and placed her hands on the ground behind her, powering into a back flip that carried her away from him, before pivoting on her heel, the need to see him—be close to him—overwhelming. "I'm sorry."

He bounced forward, leaping into the air, one leg curving high over her head as she went into a crouch. "For the invitation?" He landed. Spun toward the other side of the circle.

She had to wait for him to return to give her response. "No."

They advanced and retreated again and again, demonstrating kicks, turns and other techniques, but each time they came together, one of them brought a new message.

"Sorry for what?"

"Being stubborn."

"You are."

"I know."

The next time Clay passed, his hand brushed across hers, making the move look planned. "Why am I here?"

Come on, Marcos. Call time. I need to tell him the truth.

He came by again. "Why, Tess?"

She couldn't do this. Not anymore. So she stopped dead, right in the center of the *roda*. No longer moving to the beat. No longer putting on a show. Her eyes were centered wholly on Clay, who took one look at her and ceased all movement, as well. They stared at each other across the circle as the rhythm instruments faltered, the clapping and singing dying away a section at a time.

Then Clay was striding over to her and taking her by the shoulders. "Tell me, Tessa."

"You're here…because I want you to be. I love you."

The whole circle went silent.

"God. I never thought I'd hear you say that." His hands cupped her face. "I love you, too. But we need to be able to help each other—both of us. I need to be able to do things, without you considering it charity and pushing me away."

Hope soared in her chest.

"I know. I'll try. I'll have to, because I think I really am pregnant." She gave him a wry smile, knowing she would be battling herself about accepting his help but knowing it was a fight she had to win. And she would. Because Clay was worth it. And so was the precious life that might be growing inside her.

"You are?"

"I think so."

His eyes closed, and he pressed his forehead tight against hers in a way that made her eyes sting and her breath stick in her lungs.

"I want marriage," he said.

"Can we discuss it?"

An exasperated chuckle met her ears. "Can we compromise?"

Slowly, very slowly, she hooked her right foot behind his calf and swept his legs from under him. Down he went onto the mat, with her right beside him.

"Yes," she whispered. "We can compromise."

With that, her lips met his in front of God and everyone, handing him a promise that was stronger than any legal document. She knew he'd want to marry her eventually—Clay was old-fashioned that way. But they could talk about the timing. She wanted to get through her residency first, but after that...

After that, she'd gain not only a husband but his sweet daughter in the process.

In the background, she became aware of a dull roar that began to gather strength. The sound of clapping, and shouting. Not just from the circle of *capoeiristas* but from the crowd, who'd watched the whole strange scene unfold. She pulled her lips from his with an embarrassed laugh, only to have him slide his fingers behind her head and draw her back down. "Don't worry, Tessa, I'll wait until we get back to my house to finish this. But I fully intend to."

A shiver of anticipation rolled over her.

"Where's Molly?"

"With Mom and Dad. They're here somewhere, but they've promised to keep her for the night." Clay climbed to his feet, helping her up and then swinging her into his arms. Members of the crowd hooted its delight at the unexpected turn of events.

If she'd thought those collection jars in the hospital had been outrageous after a simple kiss, she hated to imagine what would be drawn on them next.

It didn't matter. Because, whatever it was, it would be the truth.

The musicians suddenly began beating out a frenzied rhythm while the rest of the group reacted by doing volleys of leaps, handstands and whatever other acrobatics they could fit in the now-crowded ring. From across the staging area Marcos gave her a quick wave and Brazilian thumbs-up sign of victory, just before Clay turned and carried her away from the crowds. Away from the music. Toward a future filled with fresh beginnings.

This time their match would be a lasting one, because it would be built on hard work, mutual respect and compromise. And soon, very soon, she hoped another adventure would come their way.

A new little *capoeirista*, ready to join the world of music, *rodas*…and love.

* * * * *

Don't miss the next story in the fabulous
NEW YORK CITY DOCS *series*
SURGEONS, RIVALS…LOVERS
by Amalie Berlin
Available now!